The Sheikh's C

Chapter One

Sheikh Hamid Al Wahed let loose with an elated shout as he pushed his champion camel into a gallop, leaving his mounted guards behind in his dust. Well, sand. *Whatever!* Nothing right now could contain his happiness. Even his grin had to be eating up his face when one of his random hair plaits caught in his mouth.

He blew it free with another heady laugh. Now this was living!

He'd never be a strait-laced traditionalist. Even wearing the ghutra headdress was a rare occurrence. That it not only protected his face and neck from the desert heat, but also kept his hair covered and out of the way concerned him little. He loved the bite of the sun on his scalp and the wind's hot breath against his skin while his hair was free to do whatever the hell it wanted.

He'd never conformed. He was a full-time ladies' man and a part-time drunk. And a sheikh in name only.

Little wonder his people despaired of him.

The adrenaline rush faded along with his smile, but the desert continued to speed past as his camel galloped up one sand dune and down the next.

Hamid's energy shift happened just as fast as he sank into gloomy thoughts. It was almost laughable that he'd become sheikh of Imbranak via default.

It had been his eldest brother, Ardon, whose role it had been to rule the small but ridiculously wealthy nation. Ardon who had prepared his whole life to become the next sheikh and serve his people...until the helicopter he'd piloted had crashed in the desert, killing him instantly along with his closest guards and advisors.

Hamid have never wanted or asked for the position of ruler. He'd always been a misfit by nature and—when not bedding a beautiful woman or women—a loner by choice. He craved solitude whenever he could get it.

Just like now.

Not even his favorite harem girl, Ranna, could have pulled him out of the despairing funk he was about to fall into once again.

He slowed the camel into a long, loping walk. "Good work, Camille. You've given me some space, if only for a few more minutes." Camille responded with a hoarse bellow and he nodded and said, "Glad you understand. And yes, I am rather thirsty now, thank you."

He pulled a flask from out of his thobe's pocket, then gulped down some fiery mouthfuls of arrak, the date liquor he'd become rather fond of. Though his preference to forget his responsibilities was sex with any number of his women, a mind numbing drink would also do in a pinch.

Both were preferable.

He capped his flask and shoved it back into his pocket. In a perfect world he'd be surrounded by his exotic harem women. In an even more perfect world those same women wouldn't act like puppets trained to remind him exactly who he was at every opportunity.

Ugh. It galled him no end that they spoke his name with such reverence and worshipped him like some ancient deity every time they scraped into a bow or yielded to his every perverted need.

He might love sex but sometimes he really did prefer to be alone in a Bedouin tent in the middle of the desert over the suffocating faithfulness of his servants, advisors, guards and harem women.

That they all resided in his sparkling palace with its gold-plated walls and fountains which gushed water while the sun scorched the barren earth outside its walls, left him with no choice but to occasionally escape where no one could find him.

The Sheikh's Captive Lover
Mel Teshco

He might endure the title of sheikh, but he had very little interest in public relations, politics and game playing. It was only his advisors and his surprisingly keen instincts that saw his country continue to prosper.

His lips twitched just a little. Perhaps his best friends, Mahindar, Fayez and Jamal's influence had rubbed off on him? Because, unlike Hamid, they were passionate about ruling and bringing their nations forward like no other sheikhs before them.

His thoughts drifted to his smitten friend, Mahindra, whose mind was sharper than a rapier. When that man wanted something, nothing held him back. Not even a war had managed to keep him away from Arabelle, the woman he loved.

Of course Hamid was pleased for his friend's happiness, but there was a part of him that was a little envious, too. How must it feel to love someone so unconditionally and exclusively?

Hamid had never once freely given his heart to a woman. His preference was to share his love around, or at least, share his body around. But perhaps if the right woman appeared, one who didn't think he was the sun, the moon and the stars because of his sheikh status, he'd reconsider...everything.

He heaved out an aggrieved breath. At least he wasn't alone in being alone. Fayez and Jamal were still happily single. His lips quirked. He had strong doubts either one of them would be building a ballroom with its black and white checkered floor anytime soon.

Hamid still chuckled that his best friends had fallen for his drunken bet a few years ago in a game of blackjack. They clearly thought he'd lose. They might be brilliant strategists and intelligent when it came to advancing their countries, but surely they should have known better than to bet against their street smart and savvy friend?

Had they forgotten about his earlier bet, which he'd also won? It'd been hilarious watching them compete in a camel race in nothing but their birthday suits and anxious faces. That his belly laugh had been far too short-lived had had him thinking up a far more impressive scheme for his next bet, one that would continue for years to come.

Building a grand ballroom for any of them brave or foolish enough to fall in love and marry had come to him after he'd visited a wealthy sheikh with said pretentious ballroom. Hamid had spent seven hours inside that ballroom bored out of his skull, the loud orchestra piercing his ears and the overdressed people with their fake smiles and heavy jewelry hurting his eyes.

Thank heavens he'd at least had the good fortune of taking two gorgeous ladies to bed for the night; otherwise the whole experience would have been little better than watching paint dry.

But he'd decided well before those ladies had brightened his mood that his friends should have to go through the same ordeal, and from there his plan had hatched.

Of course his friends had all scoffed at the bet until Mahindar had fallen in love with the one and same woman he pledged to marry. He'd soon after commissioned an architect to build his grand ballroom with checkered black and white flooring.

And without not one word of complaint.

But Hamid was certain his smitten friend would have built a dozen new ballrooms just to be with his wife.

Camille crested the next sand dune with another bellow, pulling Hamid out of his introspection even as a flash of dusty, metallic red caught his peripheral vision. The sedan—a ridiculous choice for driving in the desert—was pulled to the side of the road AKA goat track that snaked around the dunes.

"Just the diversion I need," Hamid announced to his steed.

Taking another glug of date liquor from his flask, he ignored the distant shouts from his guards and pressed Camille into a fast gallop toward the car.

Chapter Two

Holly Petersen left her precious Nikon camera inside the slightly cooler interior of the sedan as she climbed onto its roof and held up her cell phone in the vague hope she'd get a signal. *Nothing.*

Pushing back her banana-yellow bandana that clashed perfectly with her bright red hair, she pressed a hand to her damp brow. What had she been thinking to drive alone in the desert? Her stubborn independence was going to get her killed, and her body possibly never recovered with the local people no doubt imagining she deserved her fate.

Thank goodness her practical sandals were a deterrent against the baked-in heat on the metal of the car or her feet would be cooked by now.

She shielded her eyes from the relentless sun and peered up at the nearest dune. Perhaps she'd get a signal from there? She squinted, her heart in her throat at the distant speck that quickly grew larger. Surely she wouldn't be seeing a mirage just yet? But the camel that loped effortlessly down the dune and its rider that stuck to its back with even less effort was surely real?

It was only when the camel bellowed and grunted as it gained its footing on level ground, before its rider stopped next to Holly, that she knew for certain she wasn't seeing things. The camel and its rider were all too real.

She locked eyes with the man whose dark, intense gaze trawled across her like she was the first woman he'd seen in years.

She swallowed hard, her nipples pebbling beneath her yellow kaftan. She only hoped the black beading on its bodice would conceal any illicit thoughts. Good grief, the man was clearly a savage, with his overlong hair and haphazard plaits, his stubble that was almost a beard and his sweaty, sandy skin.

Her throat dried and her pulse stuttered. *Shit.* What were his intentions? If he was a savage she'd expect no help. She took a backward step, closer to the edge of the sedan's roof. He *was* dangerous. She knew that now. And she'd been beyond foolish to trek around the Middle East alone.

But how else could she prove herself as a freelance photographer if she had to bribe a team to go along with her? Not that she could ever afford such a luxury anyway. She was just beginning her career after leaving Australia almost three months ago.

The itch to photograph the man who sat so nonchalantly on his camel, the same man who also exuded such dangerous intensity was too irresistible for her artistic brain. Putting up a placating hand, she said, "If you wouldn't mind staying just like that for a minute, I would love to take a photo of you."

His eyes narrowed and gleamed, but he said nothing as she clambered awkwardly from the sedan's roof. Dropping her phone on the driver's seat, she reached inside for her camera, placed its strap around her neck then clambered awkwardly back on the roof.

Lifting the camera, she took some shots of the man sitting astride his camel. With a scowl, he issued an order that had the camel drop obediently to its knees and then onto its haunches. The rider then slipped gracefully out of the carved saddle and onto the sand in his sandals and thobe, and approached her with flashing eyes.

He gestured at her with clear, universal signals that communicated she stop taking his photo. She ignored him. Her whole body hummed, excitement and delight surging through her. This was a once in a lifetime opportunity! He was a nomad living in the desert, surviving in one of the harshest landscapes in the world! And these shots were magnificent, amazing!

Her finger was still busy clicking when he jumped lithely onto the roof and all but ripped the camera off her neck and out of her hands. His dark, swarthy face was red with rage, his eyes bleak and his breath boozy. "No. More."

Those two words were filled with angst and throbbed with danger. And her damn body responded to his alpha maleness like a headstrong mare did to a hot-blooded stallion.

It's just the adrenaline of the photos, nothing more, a little voice reasoned.

Yeah, right.

Already the man, whose headdress was noticeably absent, held the camera in one big, callused hand like it was an explosive and he was about to throw it out of harm's way. She shivered. That he was also a little inebriated meant there might not be any talking sense into him.

She had personal experience in that regard. Her dad had been an abusive alcoholic whose one true love was the bottle. That her mother had become a withdrawn, drab gray mouse scared of her own shadow had been Holly's biggest influence in life.

Her bright red hair might be natural, but her even brighter clothes reminded her to never allow someone to strip away any color or joy from her life. All she wanted was her freedom and the right to capture the world—the colorful and the dreary and everything in-between—with her camera.

She shook her head as his arm flexed, ready to throw away her most precious possession. "No. Don't destroy my camera." she managed a smile, though her voice came out stupidly husky. "It's all I have in the world and the only reason I'm even here."

His lip curled at her words, like he blamed the camera for her predicament. "Then you're a fool," he muttered, before he threw the Nikon high into the air. It bounced on the nearby dune, then rolled and finally lay still in the sand.

Horror for a moment left her disabled. Then something flicked a never-before-seen-madwoman switch inside her. *"No!"* she screamed. She beat her fists against his chest even as her tears came and she sobbed as she hit him, over and over again.

It was only once she was seriously weakened and resigned to her fate that she realized they weren't alone. A dozen camels and their riders stood around the broken down car, some of the men's faces revealing utter shock and others furious looks of disgust.

"Come," the man she'd repeatedly hit said in a neutral tone. Like she'd had no more strength than a gnat and was just as annoying. "You are clearly dehydrated and out of your head."

She scowled. How dare he assume such a thing, as though his throwing her beloved camera to the ground wasn't enough to set her off! "I'm not going anywhere with you."

He shrugged. "Then you will die alone out here in the desert, your bones picked clean by scavengers."

She didn't wait for him to coax her into leaving with him. Dropping from the car roof, she scampered partway up the dune to grab her camera where it lay. She pursed her lips and blew off the grains of sand. It didn't appear to be broken. She sagged. There really was a God! Placing the strap around her neck she held the device protectively against her chest as she turned, prepared to snarl abuse at the career wrecker.

But if she thought he'd be waiting for her she was sadly mistaken. She gaped as the savage and his friends turned their camels around and headed away from her.

Slipping awkwardly down the bank of sand, she jogged after them, her focus on the lead, bareheaded rider. "Where the hell do you think you're going?" When he and his men ignored her and continued on their merry way, her jog turned into a sprint and her budding anxiety turned into a whirlwind of rage. "Hey. *Hey!* What the fuck *is* this?"

The camels moved into a trot, the leader of the ragamuffin bastard club sitting astride his stead with his half-a-dozen black plaits bouncing. She gritted her teeth and stopped. Then lifting her camera she took dozens of photos of the retreating asshats.

"Best shots ever!" she screamed out. "The people of this country are going to love reading about the men who left behind the lone woman to rot in the desert. I can't wait to share these photos around!"

Her tension faded as the camels slowed and finally stopped. The lead camel with its horrid rider sitting astride then turned around and trotted back toward her.

"Yeah, I thought that might get your attention," she said fiercely, one hand on her hip and the other cradling her camera.

The man stopped his camel in front of her. It made a baleful sound as it once again stooped obediently to its knees then dropped its backend, its rider rocking in the saddle. He eyed her critically, his dark stare unreadable.

She shifted uncomfortably. Yes, she was a hot mess, who wouldn't be under the desert sun that drained every particle of moisture from the body? It wasn't as if he was an oil painting, either!

He was a drunken savage!

Except the camera didn't lie. Every shot she'd captured of him had showcased a maverick, a savage of a man who was as one with the barren landscape and his damn camel. That his shrewd eyes hid secrets and a brilliant mind even now sent little shivers down her spine. *Fuck.* She wasn't some wet-behind-the-ears virgin. She'd had her share of lovers.

That not one of them had affected her as profoundly as this desert native was nothing more than her artist's eyes picking up on his charisma, his larger than life presence.

Too bad he was a drunk! He'd had the nerve to call her a fool, yet what person in their right mind didn't keep up their hydration in the desert? Everyone knew alcohol dehydrated the body!

She shook her head and glowered. "What is this? A standoff?

"You want to come with me—then come. If you don't, then do not run after me screaming like a banshee."

She blinked. "What? So you want me to climb behind you on th-that thing?"

His dark eyes glittered, his lush, sexy lips tightening. "Last. Chance."

"Fine." She stomped toward the beast that eyed her as warily as she eyed it. "Where do I sit?" She looked at the padded, artfully engraved wooden saddle with its striped, colorful cloth beneath. Thank goodness she'd worn leggings beneath her kaftan. "You surely don't intend for me to sit behind you squished like a sardine?"

He sighed heavily, and she quickly slid behind him before he changed his mind and left her to fend for herself. She blinked at the warm seat and the even warmer body in front of her. *Damn.* His scent was an oddly luxurious mix of citrus and frankincense.

"I suggest you wrap your bandana around the lower half of your face beneath your eyes."

She grudgingly did as he asked. She had fair skin and the bandana would help stop a lot of the sunburn. She was only grateful that her hair would shield her nape at least.

"Hang on," he commanded.

She wasn't about to touch his hot, sweaty body. Placing her hands behind her back, she clung onto the lip of the saddle.

"Arms around me," he ordered brusquely. "Unless you plan on tipping off the moment the camel stands."

She threw her arms around him, shuddering at his sinewy, powerful body. She was used to softer men who cooked in kitchens, worked in offices or taught in classrooms. Unlike this hardened, desert man. Even beneath his thobe it was obvious he had not an ounce of fat on him. She closed her eyes. She'd bet the only fat he sported was between his—

She shrieked as the camel pushed to its feet, the ungainly rocking motion snapping her neck forward to crack her brow against the back of the savage's head, before her neck snapped back and the world righted itself again.

She resisted rubbing her brow and giving him ammunition to imagine her some pitiful, weak damsel in distress.

"Are you okay?" he asked gruffly.

She might have been if it wasn't for the smirking stares that practically burned into her back from his men. "I've been worse, I'm sure," she said ungraciously. "Now if you could hurry and get us to the nearest city, I'll be a whole lot better."

She expected many things, but not the short, sharp burst of laughter from his mouth, his shoulders for a moment shaking with mirth. "You are too funny," he said, then urged his camel back around to where his men waited.

"What is so funny about that?" she gritted, vaguely insulted by his mirth even as she was fascinated by it. To have photographed him in full laughter would have made her day. Instead her camera was wedged between her breasts and his back.

He turned his head to look at her, his dark eyes assessing hers. That was when she noticed his ridiculously long lashes, absurd really, for a man. Her red-gold lashes faded into obscurity unless she used oodles of mascara.

He sighed. "I'm saving your life. Let's just leave it at that."

"And I'm grateful," she said, "I really am. But I'm not rolling in money, okay? I don't owe you anything." She glanced at the hostile men ahead. Weren't they the same men who'd been amused at her expense just a few seconds ago? She cleared her throat. "I don't owe any of your men one red cent."

When the rider—she guessed she was a pillion passenger—burst out laughing once again, the other men glanced with grinning speculation and surprise at one another. Her stomach contracted and she bristled. Was she nothing more than the butt of his jokes?

"I'm glad I amuse you," she said frostily. "Or do you treat all women with this superior level of condescension!"

"No." The savage barely withheld his amusement. "Only you."

He commanded his camel into a trot while his men's laughter echoed in her ears and left her face hot, and with no choice but to grip onto the maddening leader's waist or risk falling to the ground.

Chapter Three

Hamid couldn't remember the last time he'd enjoyed himself so much. The girl—no, the *woman*—pressed behind him was both alluring and entertaining. She fascinated him with her red-gold hair, sparkling green eyes and vivacity for life. Not to mention her zero decorum.

How nice to battle wills with a woman who wasn't afraid to speak her mind. A woman who didn't scrape and bow and who clearly had no idea who he was. He intended to keep it that way, too.

He'd already taken his men out of earshot while she'd retrieved her camera to tell them not to speak with her lest they give him away. He wanted to stay an anonymous stranger and bask in the experience of being an equal.

But as the first mile became ten he vacillated between desire with her breasts squished enticingly against him and distress from the damn camera chafing his skin below his shoulder blades.

No harem girl he'd ever met put their own possessions above his comfort. They knew better...were trained to alleviate his every ache, including the throbbing ache between his thighs.

That this soft western woman with her distinct Australian twang for an accent hadn't yet complained blew his mind. He imagined her tender, pale skin would be burned to a crisp from the bright sun, her flesh bruised and battered with the rubbing motion of the saddle from the camel's every stride.

He supposed not every female was fragile and delicate, just as not every Australian woman was a deeply-tanned, blonde surfer who lived in the sun.

"What is your name?" he asked gruffly.

13

She shifted a little behind him, then said weakly, "Holly. Holly Petersen."

"Holly, would you mind removing the camera embedded in my back?"

One of his men sniggered and Hamid turned a baleful eye at Essam. The man couldn't quite hide his twitching smirk, though he did a fair impression of respectfully turning his head away. His men were no doubt thanking Karma for his discomfit after he'd left them behind and had his safety compromised.

He sighed in relief as she plucked the camera from the indent in his back. Perhaps he *had* been foolhardy escaping from his men for a handful of blessed minutes. But he had no regrets. Not even for bringing this woman into his camp.

As Sheikh of Imbranak he was risking much by keeping this single western woman in his tent. If the news leaked it wouldn't go down well with his people at all. *Too bad.* He refused to leave her alone to possibly die. The heat and lack of water weren't the only things to fear in the desert. Marauders, snakes, scorpions and hungry predators roamed the area.

His whole body tensed. She was too trusting. He could have as easily been one of the many brigands living in the desert. The depraved groups of men were little more than felons and would have happily shared her around to all the men to satisfy their urges.

So what are you planning for her?

He drank deeply from his skin, the date liquor sending a nice burn to the pit of his stomach. She was no harem woman. She was a headstrong westerner with her own views and ideals. And that was what probably fascinated him the most.

His cock twitched yet again at the thought of taming her, then having her cry out in surrender as he buried his cock deep between her creamy thighs. He stifled a groan. He'd been in the desert for five days and intended to stay another five. He only managed to get away every three or four months, which meant he rarely went without sex for more than a few days.

What he'd do right now to have his favorite harem girl, Ranna, waiting in his tent for him. He'd even forgive her for worshipping the ground he walked on as long as she worshipped his dick with the same level of enthusiasm.

Anything to relieve the growing pressure in his groin.

So why did his mind immediately envision a green-eyed, red-haired woman beneath him? He rolled his eyes. He really must be sexually deprived. Either that or he was giving into the fantasy of having a woman treat him like any other man.

That his cock was a pillar of stone and his balls rubbed raw on the saddle from their inflated size didn't dim his urge to take her one bit.

"And your name?" she asked.

Thank heavens her question took his mind off all thoughts of sex. "Hamid."

"Hamid," she repeated softly. "I've heard that name before."

His pulse surged into double beats. He only hoped she didn't ask for his full name. "It's common enough."

"Where I'm from names like John and James are common."

He smirked. What had he been worried about? She had no clue of his identity. In fact, he got the distinct impression she thought him some desert rat who rarely, if ever, ventured out from his corner of the desert.

Not only had he had a western education, he'd travelled the world many times and was well aware of how common John and James were as names in the western world. He'd even been good friends with more than a few of them over the years.

Camille climbed the final dune, the small valley below with its oasis of blue sparkling water and date palms coming into view. His tent was pitched close to the water, where the shade from the palms helped keep it cool. The camels had their own roped enclosure well away from the tent on the other side of the oasis, where green tufts of grass edged the water.

His men had also set up a basic camp near the camels, where they kept an eye on the animals as well as any possible intruders. The kitchen fly—a tent without walls—was halfway between both the men's camp and Hamid's tent to give him the solitude he craved.

"Wow," Holly breathed. She leaned around him. *Click. Click. Click.*

"No more photos!" he snapped, surprised when this time she actually obeyed.

But not without protest.

"What a killjoy," she grumbled.

He resisted snorting. He was known to be the life of the party. The man who drank too much, womanized even more, and gambled to keep things interesting. Anyone in his circle knew killjoy was the opposite of him. He lived for pleasure and those momentary flashes of fun.

He grimaced. Holly would probably despise the real him.

When he stopped Camille next to the tent and commanded her to kneel, Holly moved with the jerky motion so that she didn't bash her head with his. He grinned. "You'll make a camel rider yet."

That she stumbled as she got out of the saddle showed her level of fatigue, and he frowned as he dismounted, then drew her close before leading her into his tent while his men led Camille away for a much needed rest.

He inhaled Holly's scent of honeysuckle vanilla even as he noted how perfectly her curves fit against the harder lines of his body. If he didn't know better he'd think she was made for him.

Except he had more important things to worry about other than their compatibility. Her pale skin was terribly sunburned and she walked stiffly, as though her whole body hurt. That she hadn't made one complaint and didn't question his ethics both warmed and concerned him.

Did she have no natural fear of what men might do to her or was she always this blindly trusting?

He pulled out his flask and tipped the last of the arrack down his throat. Except the date liquor didn't have quite the same effect as it usually did. He capped the flask and tossed it onto the pile of cushions and the mat on the floor where he slept, then headed to the filtered water that he kept inside.

"You must be thirsty," he said.

"Parched."

Guilt lanced through him. He should have thought more about her needs and less about his own. But he'd been too busy imagining every conceivable sexual position he could take her while her throat had no doubt been ragged and raw with thirst.

He filled a metal cup with the clean water and handed it to her. "Drink it slowly," he advised.

She put her camera down carefully, then removed the material around her nose and jaw before closing her eyes as she sipped the water. It gave him a chance to look more closely at her bright red skin. Luckily there was plenty of Aloe vera plants growing wild in the sand and rocky parts of the desert. Not to mention the potted plant he kept at all times in the corner of his tent.

He'd pushed his luck too many times while roaming out in the desert. The sap of the Aloe had been the only thing to bring him any relief. Stalking to the plant, he broke off a leaf and returned to Holly. "Stay still," he commanded, squeezing out some sap then gently massaging it into her skin, paying particular attention to her forehead.

His throat thickened along with other parts of his anatomy. She had such soft skin, and even sunburned she was pale as a lily. He should have covered her up more and given her fluids. But he'd become too grudgingly used to women looking after his every need, not the other way around.

"That is so soothing," she said softly. "Thank you."

"You have very fair skin, I'd hate to see it blistered." He smeared a double dose of sap on her face. Not even the material of her bandana had fully kept the sun out. "You will probably peel a little, but this will help to hydrate your skin and heal it faster."

She blinked up at him. "I'm beginning to think you're not the savage I first imagined."

"Compliments now? Dare I believe it?"

She smiled. "Just don't go getting too used to it."

Something within melted a little and he dropped the thick, spiky wedge of Aloe to cup her face in his hands. She didn't resist when he leaned down and kissed her soft, full lips. Instead she moaned a little in response, her passion surging while his became a wild animal wrenching against the tight leash he'd kept on it from the moment he'd seen her like some fearless, red-haired warrior on the roof of her car.

That the sparks of electricity shooting through him made him feel more alive and self-aware than he'd ever felt before caused him to stumble back in shock. What was going on? He'd never experienced this level of need in his life. That he was primed and ready to take her like some desert beast wasn't going to do him any favors.

Her shining eyes dulled a little. "What's the matter? Did I do something wrong?"

He resisted snorting. "You did everything right. But I don't want—"

"You don't want me?" she interjected.

No. I don't want to take advantage of you like some raging beast.

But maybe she didn't need to know that. Maybe she didn't need to learn that he was already a little bit invested in her, and that he'd never been so thoroughly intrigued by a woman like her before in his life.

He schooled his mouth into a smile and took another step back. "Get some sleep. You must be exhausted."

Chapter Four

Holly watched as Hamid spun on his heel and left the large tent as though his feet were on fire. Her stomach cramped with hurt and her eyes burned with unshed tears.

How dare he treat her like a sex object one moment and nothing the next! She'd seen that same pattern—though admittedly far worse—in her dad's treatment of her mom. One minute he'd been conciliatory and begging for her forgiveness, telling her that he loved her and was deeply sorry for hurting her. The next he'd used her as a punching bag while calling her the most despicable names imaginable.

In the end it'd been cancer that had taken her, but Holly didn't doubt for one second it had been stress and fear that had germinated the cancer inside her. Three months later her dad had died from a heart attack, though Holly liked to believe it had been guilt and sorrow that had killed him.

It left her nauseated inside that she was attracted to Hamid. She'd read enough books to know she had to break the chains to her past. Clearly being independent, wearing bright clothes and leaving her hair its natural red wasn't enough.

Ugh. She needed to get out of here and back to civilization. That she'd left her cellphone in her car along with her purse and water had to be as stupid as driving into the desert alone. But then she hadn't been left with a lot of choice. They wouldn't have kept her alive in the desert.

She rubbed her brow, grimacing at the sting thanks to what had to be some serious sunburn. She'd also left a nice, wide-brimmed straw hat on the backseat of her car.

She looked around. Though the loosely woven material of the tent appeared to be made from traditional goat and sheep hair, the interior was surprisingly spacious and luxurious, with a thick sleeping mat on the floor and lovely big cushions piled high.

She curled her lip. No doubt he and his men had stolen the goods from some poor, unsuspecting trader. There were still nomad caravans in the desert who traveled the sands on camels and traded their wares.

She headed past a bamboo divider to find a bathroom of sorts. It was surprisingly neat and organized, with a chest of drawers storing everything from clothes and toiletries, and a mirror on top reflecting back her ghastly image.

She touched her tomato-red forehead that was almost as bright as her scraggly hair. Thank god Hamid and instructed her to cover most of her face. But she couldn't do anything about the rest of her sunburn, what was done was done. She looked longingly at the hip bath. Though what she'd give to wash the sand and sweat off her body, and shampoo and condition her hair.

Or better yet, go back to her hotel room with its leaky cold shower, which had a least kept her clean. And the lumpy, overstuffed bed that had kept her off the floor and away from scorpions, snakes and all other manner of creepy crawlies.

She paced inside the tent. How did she keep getting into these shitty predicaments? Yes, she'd been travelling alone from one city to another, but it'd been sheer bad luck that had seen her car breakdown about halfway between the two and becoming completely isolated with very little chance of anyone stumbling across her car to alert the authorities.

She crossed her arms. Even if someone did find her car they'd only need to look at the few selfies on her phone along with the picture on her license to know she was a silly foreign woman just asking for trouble out in the desert alone.

This time her luck might well and truly have ran out.

Not that she was complaining. Thanks to Hamid she had food and water. She'd survive, which was more than she could say if he hadn't come along.

Her eyes narrowed on spotting the freestanding gun cabinet that was next to the filtered water in one corner of the tent. She approached it slowly, cautiously. It was locked...of course it was. Good. She'd always despised firearms. Knowing a single bullet could kill a person made her sick to the stomach.

Turning her back on the gun cabinet, she retrieved her precious Nikon from the floor. There was only one thing left to do. She lifted the camera and focused on the sparse living area inside the tent. *Click. Click. Click.* She'd make the most of her time here and try to capture everything.

These might even be her breakout pictures!

It wasn't until she stepped outside to the magical sunset that lit up the desert and oasis of water in red and golds that she realized she had a real opportunity to portray the unique and magnificent landscape. Even the camels in their yard looked fascinating with their shadowy silhouettes in the bright foreground of water.

"Is that really necessary?"

She lowered her camera and spun around at Hamid's dark voice behind her. "It's as necessary to me as breathing," she admitted. Then raising her camera again, she took some shots of him, too. "Believe it or not you take an amazing photo."

"Enough," he said gruffly, not charmed one bit by her compliment. "It's time to eat."

He stomach chose that moment to cramp and then growl. "You have food here?" she asked weakly.

He lifted a brow. "A man's got to eat."

"Yet all I've seen is a man who likes to drink."

He smirked. "I do like a little drop of liquid nectar now and then."

She shook her head. "I'm sure you do. The trick is knowing when to stop."

He shrugged. "I stop when I've had enough."

"You know...drinking and other excesses is a sign of weakness." She tilted her head to the side. "*Are* you weak?"

He threw his head back and laughed hard, and she couldn't help but gape at his response. Her question had been a serious one yet he treated it like it was nothing more than a joke. Which was probably how he treated everything and everyone. Did he not realize that to some people the subject wasn't just personal, but touchy and devastating, too?

"Little wonder you live in the desert like a savage!" she gritted. "Society would never accept a person with such a careless attitude!"

A man in a stained white apron and crooked teeth approached from seemingly nowhere until she noticed a skin strung between some palm trees a hundred yards or so away with a basic kitchen under its roof. He held up a covered, earthenware dish in one hand and a glass carafe of drink in another. "Dinner is ready," he announced.

Hamid's laughter had already faded, and he looked almost somber when he said, "Thank you, Qaahir."

"You're welcome, your—"

"Put the food in the usual place inside the tent," Hamid interjected, "we won't be needing any arrak today."

Qaahir's eyebrows shot to the top of his forehead even as he did a slight bow. "As you wish."

She stared at Hamid. How long would his "no drinking" policy last? She'd bet no more than a day, two at most. Not that she cared. It wasn't as if he needed to impress her. "Why do these men show you so much respect?"

"You mean, unlike you?"

She ignored him. "Is it because you're in charge of sharing whatever loot you steal?"

Hamid winked. "That *must* be it. Come on, let's eat. All your questions are making me hungry."

She didn't really have a choice—not without looking like a stubborn fool—but to follow him back into the tent, place her camera within reach on the floor, then sit ungraciously on one of the many cushions that sat atop his sleeping mat.

A young boy, no older than a teenager, lit some lamps then retreated with the glass carafe of arrack—probably for the other men to drink—while the cook placed the covered dish onto the floor and poured some filtered water into cups. With a nod, he quietly withdrew to the corner of the tent, as though to ensure their meal was satisfactory.

The moment Hamid sat opposite her then lifted the lid, the delicious scents of meat and rice and spices poured free, and she forgot all about the other man. Hamid's dark eyes glinted. "I bet you're hungry."

She sniffed appreciatively, eyeing what appeared to be some kind of flatbread with yellow-colored rice and a yogurt sauce swimming with tantalizing pieces of lamb and a sprinkling of pine nuts on top. She blinked. He sure didn't eat like some half-starved desert rat. "This food is fit for a king."

Hamid grinned, his teeth flashing white under the torchlight. He handed her a fork. "You might prefer to use this instead of your hand."

She smiled thanks. It was traditional to eat food with the right hand, and though many Middle East people continued with the practice, she'd never been comfortable picking up hot, sticky or saucy foods. Not even when the bread was used like a parcel.

"I prefer a fork, too," he conceded.

She arched an eyebrow. "So you're *not* a desert rat?"

The cook exhaled with shock, and Hamid waved off whatever the man wanted to say. "Thank you, Qaahir. That will be all for now."

"As you say," Qaahir murmured before executing a stiff half-bow and quietly retreating from the tent.

Holly shrugged off the odd feeling that something wasn't right and instead surrendered to her hunger. She dug into the rice and meat, the yoghurt splattering. "Oops. Allow me to apologize in advance. I'm a messy eater."

"Me too," he said, scooping up a forkful and stuffing it into his mouth. He pulled off a piece of bread then and folded it over with the filling inside. "Let's get messy."

As he popped it into his mouth, she asked, "Why do I get the impression you enjoy living life without rules or judgement."

He shrugged. "It's a fair observation."

She looked down at her bright clothes. "Maybe it takes one to know one. I've never been one for following rules. Especially not when it comes to fashion."

"Don't ever change." He smiled as she blinked at him. "You're an elusive butterfly whose brightness shines amongst the sea of dark colors the women of my culture often wear."

She blinked. "I believe you just complimented me in return."

He paused from eating. "Does that surprise you?"

She frowned. "I guess it does. My first impressions of you weren't exactly complimentary."

His eyes gleamed. "Let me guess...selfish, drunk, arrogant, overbearing—"

"Those words did come to mind," she admitted. "But there was also a part of me that was grateful and thankful for you being in the right place at the right time."

He nodded slowly, his expression thoughtful. "I wasn't meant to be anywhere near where I found you," he murmured. "Destiny brought us together."

She tore off a bit of bread along with its topping. "For what purpose? It's not like we have the same future goals."

He forked some rice and meat into his mouth, his gaze watchful. "Oh?"

She grimaced. "You're a desert inhabitant. I belong in the real world with other people, capturing their lives."

Hamid held her stare. "And you can't do that here?" He snorted. "Lord only knows you've taken enough pictures."

She nodded, her voice thrumming as passion for her craft poured through her. "You have no idea how unique and beautiful this desert landscape is. Add in the oasis, the camels and the sunset, it's just magical. And my lens captured all that forever, a permanent reminder of this tiny part of the world. One magical second in time that will never be seen again."

She was heady and breathless, caught up in the words as she tried to convey her passion. That same feeling exploded through her at Hamid's dark stare.

"That one moment in time seems as ethereal as you being here in my camp," he said quietly. "Here one second and gone the next."

She popped the bread with meat and sauce into her mouth, and though the flavor was amazing, she no longer really tasted the food. She was too caught up in Hamid and his choice of words. He didn't seem the poetic type. Yet he spoke to her as though she was some divine celestial being, an angel sent to save him.

She resisted snorting. Nothing like getting carried away in the moment. She should be pressuring him into taking her back to civilization, not sharing this oddly fragile moment with him. She cleared her throat. "How long will you be staying here? I mean, do you move around like a nomad or is this your permanent camp?" She held his stare. "And when do you intend taking me back to the city?"

He brushed his hands together, his expression turning inscrutable. "So many questions. Why can't you just enjoy our moment together?"

"Anyone in my position would want to know when they were able to return home."

"And where exactly *is* your home?"

"You expect me to answer you when you've yet to give me any information?"

His mouth tightened, though there was a spark of what looked like admiration in his eyes. "I was planning to stay here another four or five days. But I think I might extend it now."

Chapter Five

Holly blinked at the man who was her captor. There was no denying it anymore. Hamid *was* holding her against her will. "How much longer?"

He shrugged. "A week. Maybe two."

Her stomach plummeted. "You can't make me stay here that long!"

"I'm not making you do anything, Holly. If you want to risk walking out in the desert alone, be my guest."

Self-pity flooded through her. "You'd probably laugh if I did."

"Is that what you really think?" he asked softly.

"What I think, feel or want clearly doesn't matter, does it?" She reached for her camera, placed its strap around her neck, then stood. "I've lost my appetite."

"There is no sense in wasting perfectly good food, not out here in the desert where rations often have to be enforced." He made a parcel with the rest of the bread, wrapping up the rice, yoghurt and spiced lamb inside before he popped it into his mouth with obvious enjoyment. "Qaahir could make cardboard taste like a delicacy."

She had to admit the cook was talented. That staying here longer meant that food probably would be rationed made her angry at Hamid. Did he always only ever consider his own needs? All she wanted was to feel halfway human again. "When you're done eating I'd like to take a bath. In privacy, of course."

He lay back on the mat at her imperious request and chewed slowly, thoughtfully. Only once he swallowed did he say, "A bath? That is reserved for the one day a week I use cleaning agents for my hair and skin."

She gaped. "You only bathe once a week?"

His smirk widened. "Yes. Though I do take a swim after dinner every night to clean off and refresh."

She scowled. "I'm not getting into that water! Imagine the snakes and eels and all manner of other wildlife!"

"If there are any creatures in there they won't go near us, they are more scared of us than we are of them."

"If you say so."

"Not convinced, huh. Perhaps you should be more interested in the wildlife that visits the oasis than what might nibble at your toes in the water."

"Wildlife?" she asked, her damn voice squeaking.

He grinned. "Yes. Falcons often visit. As does the Arabian sand cat, red fox and Oryx. You might even see an Arabian leopard or wolf."

"Seriously?" she whispered.

"If there is one thing I'm serious about, it's our native animals. Come for a swim with me and I'll do all I can to point the animals out for you."

She nodded, then muttered ungraciously, "Fine."

It was dark outside with the barest slither of a moon peeking out at them from up high. The only other light source was a small campfire near where Hamid's men were camped, the flames too far away to penetrate the darkness this side of the oasis.

"Don't worry, you're safe with me," Hamid reassured as she stood in her kaftan close to the water. "Leave your clothes on if you prefer, they probably need a clean anyway."

She frowned, stupidly upset that he cared less if she was clothed or naked. Despite some of the nicer things he'd said to her, he clearly wasn't that attracted to her. Not like she was to him.

She slipped the camera strap off over her head, then hung it from a stub protruding from the trunk of a date palm. Her camera was safer there than on the ground, and if an animal did by chance pay a visit—if they could see it—she'd have the camera within easy access.

Hamid whipped off his clothes and draped them over a palm leaf, and she silently cursed the darkness that left with nothing more than a vague silhouette of his nakedness.

What she wouldn't do for a flashlight right now.

Damn. How long had she been without a man? Too long, apparently.

Water splashed and he called out. "Are you just going to stand there or are you coming in?"

"I'm coming," she mumbled, her face immediately heating at the wishful words that echoed her traitorous thoughts. She'd like to be coming underneath him, which showed how desperate she was getting. That he was a desert rat was one thing, that he was verging on alcoholism was another.

She would *not* be like her mother!

She slipped off her sandals. The moment her bare feet touched the cool water she sighed, her internal debate forgotten.

It was far nicer than she'd imagined, the cool water soothing her burned skin. She followed Hamid, her feet sinking into the sandy bottom. She walked as deep as her hips, then crouched so that she and her clothes were almost fully immersed. It was nothing short of blissful having the cool water settling around her sore body.

"Good?" Hamid asked, crouching low too as he turned back to her.

"I might want to stay in here forever."

He chuckled. "Be careful what you wish for."

She smiled. "You're right. With my skin I'd be a prune before I knew it."

He moved toward her. "We need to protect your skin at all costs."

"Says the man who doesn't even wear headgear."

He snorted. "I'm not very traditional in that regard. But I have naturally olive skin while you have—"

"Pale white skin and red hair. You don't need to tell me. It's been my curse for as long as I can remember."

"A curse?" he murmured, suddenly in front of her. He lifted his wet hands to cup her face. "Your hair and skin are magnificent."

It was as if his touch flipped a switch inside. Her breathing grew ragged and choppy, her senses on high alert. He might have been the only man in the world right then. Even the muttering of the men around their campfire was muted to a barely legible background noise.

It was just Hamid and Holly.

And the glinting stars that bejeweled the dark sky above.

She closed her eyes as his head moved close and his lips closed over hers. Thank heavens she'd covered her nose and mouth with her bandana and her lips weren't chapped, or she might have missed the sensation of Hamid's soft, yet demanding mouth claiming hers.

One of his hands moved to the back of her head, keeping her in place as they kissed. She sighed into his mouth, her body set adrift in a marvel of awareness. It was like a fairytale and a dream all rolled into one, the water cocooning them in an enchanted bubble.

Why had she never felt this attuned before with another man? It was as if the world was spinning backwards and the stars were pin-wheeling behind her eyes. Never mind that she was hundreds of miles away from civilization. Being with this man made everything right.

It was Hamid who pulled back first, and she bit back a disappointed moan as she locked onto the faint gleam of his eyes. "My apologies," he said.

"Whatever for?" she asked bluntly.

"For taking advantage of you while you're sore and vulnerable."

She moved back toward him. "I might be sunburned and aching from the camel ride, but otherwise I'm fine. I'm an independent woman, Hamid. I've been with other men. If I want sex, I have it. I most certainly won't apologize for it."

His breath hissed. *"Do* you want sex with me?" he asked hoarsely.

She nodded, then smiled at the realization he probably didn't see it. Except he must have, because one moment he was inches away from her, the next he was close and scooping her into his arms, and kissing her as he waded back to shore.

He only pulled his mouth away from hers when he set her down outside his tent and helped her to drag off her wet clothes. She giggled a little at the urgency that left them dropping her clothes to the sandy ground before he tugged her inside the tent and flicked the fleecy door shut behind them to give them privacy.

The torchlight glinted and flickered, making everything seem surreal, especially his nakedness.

He was flawless. Lean and tough, with sculpted shoulders revealing long hours in the saddle and the hard work that came with it. His narrow hips showcased strong thighs and a cock that seemed larger than life, pulsing and hard.

"I take it you like what you see?"

"Not bad," she croaked.

His smile ate up his face, his eyes admiring her right back. "You're a porcelain doll," he murmured. "Exquisite in every way."

He took her in his arms again, then lowered her onto the mat on his floor before he followed her down, and reached into a pouch beside one of his many cushions to withdraw a condom.

She blinked up at his face. Just how many women was he prepared to screw out here in the middle of the sand dunes?

But then he deftly put on his condom and bent to kiss her again, and all questions faded into the nether as she succumbed to his expertise.

The wet, silken slide of their heated skin-on-skin contact was emphasized somehow by the nudging of his pulsating cock against her while his powerful body framed hers. Then he reached between her thighs and thumbed her hypersensitive clit. She jerked at the electric sizzle, her clit engorging at his touch.

"So sensitive," he murmured near her ear. Then, "Let's see just how sensitive you really are."

It took her a moment to realize he was already sliding down her body and pressing kisses along the way. She shivered when his lips, his warm breath, and the tip of his tongue awakened erogenous zones she never knew she had. That place between her collarbone and throat. The dip of her navel and the indent near each of her hips. When his head finally stopped between her thighs, she was quivering all over and spread apart for him in open invitation.

"So gorgeous," he murmured, his head canted back and his eyes heated. Then he moved into position so he was level with her inner pink flesh and she was exposed and vulnerable to a man like she never had been before.

Oh, she'd enjoyed oral sex more than a few times, but it'd been far more impersonal, usually in the dark and without this heated, lingering appraisal.

Hamid made her feel empowered though, not awkward, like he was worshipping her even before he touched—

She gasped and jerked as the tip of his tongue stroked the underside of her plump clit. His big, calloused hands curled around the top of her thighs to hold her in place. Then he licked her clit around and around, his rotating tongue creating hot sparkles of pleasure that escalated with intensity before setting her off like a firecracker.

But he wasn't done. The moment her orgasm faded he placed his whole mouth over her flesh and suckled hard. She screamed at the effervescence that lit her up from the inside out and took away all sanity, careless even to the fact that her response no doubt had been easily heard in this desert landscape.

She was drifting then, savoring every second of bliss and still too high to make out his murmured words while she gently floated back down to earth.

He moved back over her, and she was only vaguely aware of his head above hers and his eyes glinting with passion. He moved his hips forward and she gasped, her eyes popping wide open as he plunged inside her, his large cock filling her to the point of pain.

His smile was closer to a grimace as he looked down at her and waited for her inner muscles to loosen. "You're tight enough to be a virgin."

She was too shocked to answer. She might as well be one for how painful his entry had been. "Just how big are you?" she gritted.

He smoothed her brow with a hand, his touch cool on her heated skin. "It doesn't matter. Soon enough your pain will become pleasure."

She had serious doubts about that. Her body would never accept his size. But then he gently rocked in and out. Slowly and carefully at first, though going by his harsh breaths, straining muscles and the tic jerking at one side of his jaw, holding back was as painful for him as his entry had been for her.

It didn't take long for her body to begin to respond, incremental microbursts of pleasure that loosened her muscles and left her wanting more, until she was meeting him thrust-for-thrust and urging him on harder and faster.

She should have been prepared for the orgasm that hit her like a freight train, but she really wasn't. It threw her higher than before, straight into nirvana, where she fizzed and sparked with a burst of ecstasy that must surely have lit her up brighter than any star.

If she made any sound she wasn't conscious of it. She was only conscious of her pleasure, then of Hamid's roar as he succumbed and released deep inside her, his seed emptying into the condom.

Thank god.

She wasn't on birth control, not anymore, it'd made her too sick. It meant having to be extra careful when she had sex and always relying on other protection. She was only glad Hamid had been man enough to take care of that side of things.

She wasn't ready for children anytime soon. She'd even considered an operation so that she'd never have to worry about conceiving...never have to worry that one of her own might go through what she did.

Hamid disconnected with an unwilling grunt and disposed of his condom in the sectioned off area of the bathroom. She didn't have time to fret or second-guess having sex with him. Not even a minute later he returned, lying on the mat next to her, then rolling to face her.

One of his hands clasped the top of her leg, his other hand gently pushing some hair away from her face. "Are you okay?" he asked huskily.

She managed a laugh. "If okay means having the best orgasms of my life, then yes, I'm okay."

He chuckled, but his eyes were watchful, assessing. "The sex was great, amazing," he agreed. "And yet you seem distant."

She turned to face him fully, the flickering torchlights bringing his face in and out of focus. Light and shadow. "I was just berating myself on what might have happened if you didn't use a condom."

"Any self-recrimination is totally unnecessary. I always use protection."

She blew out a breath. "I just didn't want to end up like my mother."

"Oh?"

She swallowed at his intensity, like he knew her muttered attempt at an explanation was vitally important. She couldn't exactly back out now. Her eyes holding his she said quietly, "Stuck with a violent alcoholic."

Chapter Six

Hamid could have been struck with a sledgehammer in the gut and it still wouldn't have hurt half as much as what Holly admitted to him.

What the actual fuck? Yes, he might like his liquor, but it would never make him violent toward anyone, least of all a woman he cared about.

What sort of a life had she lived to believe every male would have cause to become violent when they drank?

"I promise you right now I would never lay a hand on you in violence."

Though he couldn't promise she wouldn't enjoy a stinging smack on the ass when they made love. He had plenty of floggers, amongst other things, where they could experiment and see how far she could be pushed. There was a wildness inside her that begged for something more than vanilla sex.

His dick stirred at the thought and he withheld a groan. He'd always loved sex but being with Holly was taking that to a whole new level. Having her beneath him, on top, sideward, and taking her from behind seemed to take up everyone one of his brain cells lately.

She sighed softly. "Promises are just meaningless words. It's actions that count."

"Then give me a chance to prove I'm a good guy." Hamid ignored his erection and held her stare. "I feel terrible knowing what your mother—what *you*—must have went through. Just please don't tar all men with the same brush as your father. Yes, I enjoy a drop of arrack. But it doesn't make me a bad man."

She bit her bottom lip. "I'm not sure it makes you a good man, either."

"I can live without arrack." The truth was an epiphany. An incredible realization he couldn't deny. He could live without arrak. But he couldn't live without Holly. Not right now.

She blinked. "You believe that, don't you?"

He nodded. "I do."

"Well...I'll believe it when I see it."

It was odd the tenderness filling him from the inside out. If it was the last thing he did it would be to prove to her that he was a man of his word. Someone trusting who she could count on.

Unlike her father.

He lifted a hand and stroked one side of her face, being mindful of her sunburn. "What do your parents think of you traveling the Middle East by yourself?"

She closed her eyes momentarily. "They would probably be shocked if they were alive. My mom died of cancer, my dad of a heart attack a few months later. But I believe my mother would have been proud of me and my independence." Her smile quivered. "She was a broken woman in the end, a shell of the woman I imagine she once was."

"I'm sorry," he murmured, little wonder she had issues. Her parents might be dead but her memories of them were very much alive. He had no doubt those memories were sharper because her mom and dad weren't around. There was nothing quite like clarity of recall when that was all one had to hold onto.

He should know.

He still remembered his older brother's charismatic energy like he was standing in the tent right now looking down at them, a sneer on his lips. Ardon had never forgiven Hamid for their mother's death after she'd died from complications giving birth to him.

A part of Hamid had believed him. It wasn't like their dad negated it. He'd been as cold to Hamid as he'd been warm to Ardon. The golden child who could do no wrong. Not even Hamid's various nannies had been able to comfort him in that regard.

At least, not until he'd been somewhere between a man and a teenager, and one young, pretty nanny in particular had shown him a comfort he'd never soon forgotten. Sex had become his buffer against the guilt that plagued him. It hadn't taken long for him to discover that liquor dissolved the guilt even more, at least for a short time.

Waking up was the worst. Because then all the self-disgust and guilt he carried became ten times worse, and he'd have to go through the whole scenario again of sex and drinking just to forget and numb the mental pain.

But though he'd been tempted a time or two, he'd never touched drugs to alleviate his anguish. He might be known as the life of the party, but he'd never be known as a drug addict.

"Don't be sorry," she said softly. "I wouldn't be here now, making love to you, if it wasn't for my sense of adventure. And it's not as if my parents' death is your fault."

He sucked in a breath, her words so contrary to what he'd heard growing up it was almost intolerable.

Her eyes widened. "Are you okay?"

He managed to crack a smile. "Yes. Of course."

Liar!

But though he could deny the truth to Holly, he couldn't deny it to himself. His mother would still be alive today if it wasn't for him. And no reminder that he wasn't responsible would heal the slash cutting his soul into pieces.

That Holly seemed to be the one and only thing to soothe his sense of loss and endless guilt wasn't lost on him. As her lashes slid closed and she dropped off to sleep, he stayed awake watching her for long hours until he too finally slipped asleep.

Chapter Seven

Holly's eyes fluttered open to mostly shadows, with only a couple of torches still flickering and spluttering, just barely illuminating the dark, watchful stare of Hamid.

She blinked at him and smiled as their lovemaking rushed back to her in stunning detail, every intimate, pornographic, pleasurable second of it. "Good morning," she croaked, sounding more like a dehydrated frog than a woman ensnared in her lover's gaze.

"Morning," he replied huskily, his voice reminding her of butterscotch drizzled over ice-cream.

Huh. Typical.

She stifled a yawn, though she'd slept like a log last night after her lovely orgasms. "What are the plans for today?"

Other than lots more sex? She shivered at the delicious notion.

"I thought we might lie in the shade near the water to see if you can capture some wildlife shots."

Her mind finally computed his suggestion and she pushed to her feet in instinctive reaction. It wasn't until his breath hissed out and his admiring eyes scanned her that it infiltrated her consciousness she was still naked.

It was a little too late for modesty now. He'd looked at and tasted her most intimate femininity. He'd also become as one with her both physically and mentally, or at least, that was how it'd felt to her. She'd never been touched emotionally like she had with Hamid.

"I should probably get my clothes," she said with a wry smile.

He shook his head. "I'm afraid our urges overtook our common sense last night." He stood, fully naked, too. "Your clothes will be sandy and damp."

He strode toward the partition that was his bathroom, his back muscles flexing and pulling with every step, his pale buttocks built to caress and clasp. He returned with a thobe, his semi-erect cock making his front even more impressive than his back.

His nostrils flared as he smiled at her, as though aware of her thoughts. As though aware that her mouth had gone dry and her pussy was now wet. He cleared his throat. "It's a men's garment and probably miles too big, but at least it will cover you while your clothes are cleaned and dried."

She nodded, and managed to pull it on. And though it really was miles too big and billowed around her, it was soft and clean and smelled of Hamid, of frankincense and vague notes of lemon.

That he was still naked didn't seem to bother him. She was more bothered when he retrieved another thobe and pulled it over his strong, lean body. It was only when he also grabbed a folded up pair of binoculars that she remembered what they hoped to achieve.

He nodded at her. "We have a few hours before breakfast. We should see something at the oasis before then."

They stepped outside to a morning that was still more night than day, with only a faint tinge of light giving any suggestion that sunrise was in the air. Hamid led her to the group of date palms, one of which still had her camera hanging from it.

Shit. She must really have been distracted to not have grabbed that before going into the tent. The Nikon was her most prized possession, one she didn't leave behind...ever. She'd managed just fine to bring it here with her while leaving behind her cellphone, water, purse and hat in the hire car.

"Just remember to aim your camera away from where the camels and my men are as no wild animal with any sense will go near them," Hamid said quietly.

She nodded as she carefully cleaned her lens on the fabric of his borrowed thobe. As she lay on her belly on the sand and grass, Hamid moved into position beside her, his binoculars in hand. He appeared to know not to talk then and it seemed as though hours ticked by before he nudged her carefully and pointed in the shallow water to their left.

She aimed her lens to where he'd indicated, holding back a gasp of delight at seeing the pale yellow leopard with its rosette fur and huge paws prowling toward the waterhole. *Click. Click. Click.* Its ears flickered at the shutter noise but it continued forward and finally crouched at the water to lap at the water.

Beautiful.

She'd read these animals were on the verge of extinction despite attempts to breed them in captivity. There was a market for their hides and other body parts that were sold on the black market.

She continued to take photos. It seemed impossible to believe that this footage might be one of the last taken of these beautiful creatures in the wild.

She'd taken close to a hundred shots of the leopard by the time it had finished drinking, then stalked away from the oasis and into the desert where the color of it's hide meant it soon disappeared amongst the dunes and sands as though it had never been.

She turned to Hamid. "I can't believe I just captured that magnificent animal."

His smile was sad. "That male is one of the few left in the wild."

She blinked at him. "You've seen him before?" At his nod she asked, "Is anything been done to save him?"

He cleared his throat. "The sheikh of Imbranak is doing his best to save him and the few remaining population of wild animals."

She snorted. "Wouldn't your sheikh be a little too busy to oversee animal preservation?"

He frowned. "What do you mean?"

She turned away and checked the waterline of the oasis through her lens. "Never mind."

"I'm interested to hear what you've heard about our great sheikh."

She lowered her camera and turned back to him. "*Great* sheikh?" She raised her eyebrows. "Is that what you and your people call him?"

"I'm guessing you've been told otherwise?" he asked quietly, his eyes holding eyes with an intensity that was a little disconcerting.

She sighed. "Look it's not for me to judge, okay? I'm a foreign woman on foreign soil. I'm not exactly welcome here by any men, let alone your sheikh."

"I've treated you well, have I not?"

"Considering I'm your captive, I guess you've been...accommodating." She smiled and conceded, "I've enjoyed your company."

His face tightened a little at the word *captive* but he didn't refute it, either. He was happy to have her in his camp—and why wouldn't he when she was given him sex?—and would only get rid of her when he'd had enough of her.

"So your problem isn't with the men of Imbranak, it's with the *Sheikh* of Imbranak?" he asked.

She cupped her camera as she studied him. He was clearly a devout follower of the sheikh. She'd have to tread carefully and not step on his toes by saying the wrong thing. "I just think he's got a nerve screwing women from every corner of the planet while those females born here have to follow rules that are outdated and barbaric at best."

Shit. Even when she tried to be subtle she steamrolled through his peoples traditions and customs with her western beliefs and ideals.

Expecting censure, she was surprised when he threw his head back and laughed. She gaped. And though half-aware of a falcon that fluttered into a panicked flight from the reeds nearby, she lifted her camera to instead take shots of her lover in his full gaiety.

Damn he was gorgeous with his dark eyes alight with mirth and his white teeth glinting against his dark stubble, his powerful body relaxed and indulgent.

He pushed her camera away with a hand and said mildly, "You don't mince your words, Holly. I like that. You truly are a breath of fresh air."

Her heart warmed at the compliment. When the air heated along with her blood, it seemed as natural as breathing for them to move together, their mouths becoming as one as they kissed.

She forgot about everything then. The big cat. The falcon. Even her camera, which she clasped weakly with one hand.

Then a camel bellowed and they broke apart like two teenagers caught in a tryst. A soft tread behind them had Hamid explode onto his feet with his hands fisting as though ready for battle.

"Essam," he said darkly, his fists unclenching.

The man, Essam—one of the men who'd been riding the camels—nodded his head. "Sorry to disturb you," he said with a glint in his eyes and a grin that communicated quite the opposite. "But we believe we've spotted a nomad tribe."

"Brigands?" Hamid asked.

Holly narrowed her eyes at the quick glance Hamid sent her, as though having her here would spell disaster. She shivered. Perhaps he was right. "Will they attack us if they *are* brigands?"

Hamid nodded. "More than likely, it's what they do. If they have enough numbers they'll attack and, if they win, they'll steal all our valuables and—"

"And?" she prompted.

"And likely use you as a trophy to be passed around." His mouth tightened. "If you survive that they'll then probably trade you as a sex slave for your unique looks."

She touched her bright red hair. "Is that your way to trying to reassure me?"

"It's the truth," he said starkly. "I won't lie to you."

"Then perhaps you should take me back to the city where I'll be safe." And where she just might dye her hair black.

He bristled, a pulse jerking into life at his jaw. "You're safe with us. I'd die before allowing anything to happen to you."

Essam sucked in a breath. "Your—"

"Enough, Essam. Just...tell me what you know about the nomads."

Essam dragged a heavy hand over the swarthy skin of his face, no doubt irritating his crooked, hooked nose. "Very little. They moved out of range before we could identify them. All we know for sure is that they had a large herd of camels and goats."

The news didn't appear to relax Hamid, if anything he seemed more troubled with his brows drawn together and his face tight. "And yet they retreated from the very water supply they need to keep their animals alive."

"They might have deduced who was staying here and decided to keep their distance," Essam suggested.

"Are you saying Hamid's reputation precedes him?" she asked with a wink. Anything to lighten the mood. Hard enough to comprehend Hamid's stark words that he'd die for her. And though of course he didn't mean it, in the heat of the moment he most definitely had.

When neither Hamid nor Essam disagreed her stomach did a slow roll. Who had she become involved with? Who had she damn well fucked? Was he even more dangerous than the desert savage she'd first imagined him to be?

Hamid turned to Essam. "Send a scout to follow the nomads and find out anything he can about who they are and what they want. He has twenty-four hours. In the meantime we'll double the guards around our camp."

Essam bowed a little. About to leave, Hamid added, "Oh, and take Holly's clothes and have someone clean them."

Holly's face heated as Essam picked up her dirty clothes without complaint and stalked off with them.

"You're embarrassed?" Hamid asked her.

She nodded. "It's seems odd for a man in this country to do a woman's laundry."

"My men do what they're asked."

She wrinkled her nose at him. "I wish I knew what you had over them."

He shrugged. "I have nothing over them. My men simply choose to be loyal to me. Come. Breakfast is probably waiting."

Her mouth watered at the spread inside the tent. Fried white cheese. Scrambled eggs. Black olives. Cucumbers, tomatoes and pita flatbread.

"Yum!'

She placed her camera in the far corner of the tent, then sat with him on his sleeping mat and shared the meal, eating until she was too full to move. She patted her stomach when they were finished. "You were right. That cook of yours really does know how to put a meal together."

"Cook?" Hamid laughed. "Qaahir is a highly trained chef."

She cocked her head to the side. "And you've managed to procure him out here in the desert?"

He popped a piece of cheese and an olive into his mouth. "Why not? Qaahir enjoys the challenge. And simple food often tastes the best."

"So you have simple tastes?"

He nodded. "I do. I like my own company. And I've always enjoyed a simple lifestyle."

"And simple, uncomplicated relationships?"

He frowned. "I would hardly call what we share uncomplicated."

"So what *are* you saying? That we're in a relationship?"

He nodded. "We've had sex, spent the night together, and enjoyed one another's company during the day. I'd like to think that counts as a relationship."

She blinked. "And when I get back to the city?"

"We'll deal with that when we have to." He pushed onto his knees and leaned across the now empty spread, capturing her lips with his. When he pulled back, his eyes shone and his voice was stark. "Let's just enjoy getting to know one another."

As though to emphasize his point, he stacked the dishes and placed them outside the doorway of their tent. Then he laid her on his sleeping mat. "I want to get to know *every* part of you," he said huskily.

She grinned up at him. "Well in that case...I'm all yours."

Chapter Eight

Once the scout caught sight of the backend of the nomad tribe disappearing into the distance toward what was another well-known oasis, everything seemed to settle into a routine for Holly and Hamid.

Early mornings became their quiet time, where they would leave the tent and lay low at the edge of the oasis for predator or prey to visit. Only once she'd taken countless photos did they return to the tent for breakfast and then inevitably make love for hours. A leisurely lunch served under the shade of a date palm saw them invariably talk for hours, and she was fascinated to discover they shared similar beliefs.

By day four though, she was beginning to get restless. As though aware time was marching on without her while she was in this desert bubble with Hamid. That the other part of her was content for the first time in years didn't bear thinking about.

They'd just finished lunch when Hamid announced, "I'm taking you someplace today where I know you will want to use your camera."

She brushed a desert ant off their picnic rug. "Really?"

He nodded, a smile quirking his lips. "It's a half-hour ride by camel. If you're no longer sore and bruised we can leave shortly."

Excitement filled her. "I'd love that. And no, I'm not sore." She winked. "Not from riding camels."

Hamid's gaze turned speculative. "My size does take some getting used to."

If it'd been any other man saying those same words she would have laughed at his immodesty, except Hamid was genuinely concerned for her and was clearly aware he was bigger than the average man. "I'm fine, really. I'm not the virgin your men seem to prize above all else."

He canted his head to the side. "That's a broad generalization. Not all men of my country value sexual innocence in their women. I'd be the biggest hypocrite of them all considering the number of experienced women back home I regularly—"

He looked away, his face as strained as his voice. "Sorry. I said too much."

His apology stretched her emotions tighter. "No, you said *just* enough."

"Holly, please don't make an issue out of this."

An issue? Like she was at fault here? She glowered. "You know what? I don't have an issue with you having other lovers. What I *do* have an issue with is that you deliberately hid them—hid the truth—from me."

"I might have omitted a few things," he conceded. "But I never once lied to you."

"There's a difference?"

He gazed at her like a scientist might examine a new species of bug under a microscope. "Let's just forget I ever said anything."

"Let's not!" She put her hands on her hips. "So where *do* you entertain your other lovers?"

He dragged a hand over his face and exhaled raggedly. "I have a...residence far away from here."

She swallowed hard as acid burned the pit of her stomach. "So the desert *isn't* your home?"

"The desert is the home of my heart."

"And does your heart also belong to any of those other women you fuck?" she asked hotly.

His face blanched. "My heart belongs to no one."

She sucked in oxygen that didn't quite seem to fill her lungs. The back of her eyes burned. "I guess I should have seen the signs."

Hamid scrubbed a hand over his face. "I didn't mean it like that."

"Yes, you did. You finally spoke the truth."

He squeezed his eyes closed, splotches of color staining his sun-kissed cheeks. "I've had many lovers," he admitted softly. His eyes opened again, their dark depths full of emotion. "But none like you."

Was that supposed to make her feel better? She'd always been different. It didn't mean Hamid—*any* man—would change their ways for her. Hell, she was only surprised he hadn't gotten drunk since bringing her here to his camp. Perhaps after this little conflict between them he would.

"Just how many other women are we talking about?" she asked.

He frowned. "Does it matter? *You* are the only woman I want now."

Her face heated. "That's because I'm the only woman here to satisfy your needs! The moment you're *home* again I'm sure you'll resume enjoying intimacy with any number of those other women."

His head reared back, his plaits dancing around his dark head. "You don't believe in us and what we have?"

She pushed to her feet and glowered down at him. "I honestly don't know what I believe anymore." She all but banged her camera against the date palm's trunk as she hung it there, then dragged off Hamid's thobe she'd taken to wearing. It was cooler and more comfortable than her one and only woman's outfit.

"Where are you going?"

"I'm taking a swim. Or is that forbidden?"

"Of course it's not forbidden. But your skin—"

"Will be just fine, thank you!"

She waded into the water, its coolness a balm to her outraged soul. Was she just another fuck in a long line of fucks to Hamid? That he'd pretended to care about her knowing he'd soon be returning to his lovers made her blood boil.

Who was he anyway? She was beginning to think he was someone far more important than a leader of some ragamuffin desert gang. It was ironic that she'd actually enjoyed spending time with him out here.

She'd liked his anonymity and the knowledge he was outside the many laws that governed Imbranak.

Except it had turned out he was no better than those sheikhs with their harems of women. And she was no more important to Hamid than those women he'd left behind to come to the desert.

Tears threatened. She'd fought so hard to be a strong, independent woman, refusing to need a man. *Ugh!* It was just a pity she couldn't run from him and leave him far behind! But she wasn't a complete moron. She might have driven a car into the desert but she sure as hell wasn't going to stumble around in one. An oasis swim was the next best thing—and if any of Hamid's men saw her in her underwear—Hamid could deal with it!

What she didn't expect was for Hamid to stand and take off his thobe. She scowled at him and his bare chest, his loose white pants somehow enhancing his tanned, sinewy arms and strong shoulders. "I'd like some privacy. Some alone time."

"And I'd like to talk."

Whatever argument she had was forgotten the moment Essam's voice rang out. *"Brigands!"*

Hamid froze. Then looking at her, he commanded, "Stay in the water. Hide yourself. *Please.*"

She was too stunned to say or do anything as he gathered up their clothes and threw them into the tent, then raced back outside with nothing but his pants on and a gun in his hand.

Chapter Nine

Holly stayed deep in the water so that though her feet touched the ground, her head was barely above water. She should probably hide amongst the reeds along certain parts of the bank, but for the moment she needed to stay put and see what was going on.

Not that she could see anything yet. Luckily she heard well enough. Gunshots sounded, along with shouts and a man's screams. Camels bellowed and a horse squealed.

She shivered. *This isn't happening. This isn't happening.* But no matter how many times she repeated the mantra in the head it was all too apparent it really was happening.

She swallowed back her fear. She shouldn't be hiding in the water like a coward. She should be taking photos of everything happening. No real photographer worth their salt would stay cowering in the water when there was footage to be shown.

It was foolhardy maybe, putting her safety at risk. But Hamid was in far more danger than she was. Her pulse raced. He was in the thick of things.

She floated on her belly toward the water's edge, doing her best to stay low and out of sight. Scanning the oasis, she pushed to her feet into a crouch and waded the rest of the way to shore, where she grabbed her camera from the tree then headed back into the water toward the reeds.

She wasn't a fighter, never would be, but she was well-versed to being witness in a war zone. Her experience had conditioned her enough to not be completely terrified by what was happening now.

In fact she was calm and focused as she pushed between the reeds and found a spot where she was hidden yet could see a good portion of the camp and what was happening.

It wasn't until she pressed the camera's viewfinder to her eye that the desert landscape really came to life. The brigands had to be twenty or thirty strong, though going by the half-a-dozen figures sitting on camels further back who were wrapped up like many-layered presents, she guessed the women didn't count as fighters.

The first wave of desert savages had already dismounted from their camels and now lay prone and bloodied on the sand. The second wave sprinted toward Hamid and his men with large knives and swords. Hamid lifted his gun into the air and released a warning shot, but the brigands continued onward.

Click. Click. Click.

It took everything she had not to shake from nerves and adrenaline. These were history making photos!

Hamid lifted his gun, aimed and fired.

One of the brigands went down clutching his knee with a gargled scream. Then another and another. There were five men on the ground when their comrades attacked Hamid and his men. It as quickly apparent they were seasoned fighters who made the brigands look like children learning how to fight. It took less than ten minutes for it to end while the last of the brigands lay wounded and moaning on the sand.

The girls on the camels looked at one another as though in disbelief, but otherwise they waited passively for whatever might happen next.

Holly couldn't press the shutter button fast enough. The scene unfolding was mesmerizing! These girls clearly believed they couldn't do anything without a man's say so and simply accepted whatever fate—what the men here—would do to them.

She continued to take pictures as Hamid looked over each of his men. None had serious injuries, just scrapes and scratches compared to the brigands on the ground. He instructed his men to take their enemies into the shade and tie them up and treat their injuries, then he and Essam approached the women on camels.

One of the women bowed and cried out, her eyes glinting somewhere between fear and awe. Hamid commanded the camels to sit and they did so with outraged bellows.

Minutes later the six women dismounted and followed Hamid and Essam cautiously toward the tent Holly had shared with Hamid. She continued clicking away even as her mind raced. Were these women going to take over their tent?

Their tent? It was Hamid's tent, not hers. She was just a visitor passing through. That he was a self-professed womanizer with six extra females to choose from meant he'd probably return her home sooner rather than later.

She should be happy!

Her hands shook a little as she looked through the viewfinder and magnetized the partially hidden faces of the women. They looked young. She didn't doubt they were pretty, too, possibly even beautiful.

The brigands had probably stolen them because of their looks.

She was lucky that Hamid and his men knew how to fight or she, too, might be part of the posse of women sitting on camels before being passed around from man to man like a prime piece of pussy for all to share.

Her stomach cramped along with her finger on the shutter. But she still managed to take some more photos as the women stepped inside the tent—the fabric door swishing shut behind them—and out of sight. But not before Hamid glanced in her direction, his taut face relaxing at seeing her.

She managed a couple more shots of Hamid's men as they dragged the wounded across the sand and into the shade where they were tied up, then she had no more energy left to give.

What was Hamid going to do with these women? What about the men who were tied up? They were clearly not going to kill them if they were attending to their injuries. She could even now hear one of Hamid's men muttering observations as he checked each prisoner and had them lined up in order from worst hurt to least so that he could work on those who needed him most.

Did Hamid not only have a chef but a medical doctor or nurse too?

She was so deep in though she didn't sense someone behind her until it was too late. A wet hand slapped over her mouth before a dark voice whispered, "Say one word and you're dead."

The sharp prick of a blade against her neck emphasized just how serious the brigand was, the warm trickle of blood on her flesh warning her to do as he said.

"Get out of the water," the brigand demanded coarsely.

She nodded, sucking in a breath when the blade nicked her deeper and more blood spilled free. It took everything she had just to keep her camera out of the water and force her leg muscles to cooperate as she pushed through the reeds and sandy bottom, the brigand sticking behind her.

Hamid stepped out of the tent, his eyes locking onto hers. He froze at the brigand restraining her, but she could see the fury pulsing deep inside as Hamid asked him, "What do you want?"

"I want my women back. And I want all my men released."

"Is that all?" Hamid mocked.

"And I want my livestock to drink their fill before we leave."

Holly flinched as the crude blade nicked her throat again and more blood leaked free.

Hamid's eyes narrowed, a pulse ticking to life at one side of his jaw. "I'll have you hunted down like an animal if you hurt her again."

Holly couldn't even see the brigand, but she could smell his sour breath, sense his hatred even as his blade loosened fractionally on her throat.

"You'll have to find me and my men first, Sheikh Hamid!" he spat.

Sheikh Hamid?

She stared at Hamid—at the sheikh?—her mind whirling. Not helped one bit by him not denying the possibility. Surely her desert rat wasn't the one and same sheikh who ruled Imbranak?

Oh, God. Little wonder Qaahir had been so shocked at her reference to Hamid—Sheikh Hamid—being a desert rat!

And that hadn't been the only clue. Her words from earlier echoed in her head. *I'm a foreign woman on foreign soil. I'm not exactly welcome here by any men, let alone your sheikh.*

Then Hamid's response. *I've treated you well, have I not?*

How hadn't she put two and two together?

Her stomach rolled as cold fingers of betrayal slipped down her spine. Why had he lied to her? What had she done to make him feel the need to hide his identity? Was that why he hadn't liked her taking his photos, in case she sold them to the media?

Everyone knew the Sheikh of Imbranak valued his privacy above all else.

Hamid didn't take his eyes off the brigand. "You still have a small chance to leave with your head on your shoulders and with any of those women who *want* go with you. But only if my woman stays unharmed."

"What about my men?" the brigand snarled.

"They will be set free. Though I can't promise some won't die from their injuries."

"Better to die an honorable death than at the hands of an enemy."

Holly would have laughed if the situation wasn't so dire. How was it okay for this one uninjured man to speak for those wounded? Was he their leader? Maybe his men preferred the chance to live rather than to die an apparently honorable death?

Hamid took a step closer. "Let my woman go and you have my word I'll do everything you have asked."

"Not until my men are freed and my camels and goats have drunk freely."

Hamid's jaw clenched as he nodded stiffly. Qaahir stepped out of the shadows to approach the men with a huge chef's knife. Some of them shrank back and cried out while others looked resigned to their fate, until Qaahir bent and cut through their bindings, leaving them unharmed and free to leave.

The leader immediately barked out, "Bring in the herd."

Two of the men who weren't seriously injured obeyed him, limping toward their camels then galloping into the desert and out of sight.

Holly curled her lip. Were his animals more important than his women?

The thought had no sooner formed when the brigand added, "Now release my women."

Hamid shook his head. "You've pushed my patience to breaking point. I've agreed to two of your requests. Now you will agree to mine. Free your captive or face the consequences of your stupidity."

"And lose my only bargaining chip? Not likely."

Hamid took another step. "I gave you my word. We both know that is law."

"Your law is different out here in the desert," the brigand muttered defensively.

"For you maybe." *Step*. "Not. For. Me."

"Fine."

Holly wasn't prepared for the shove from behind simultaneously to the blade at her throat moving away. She stumbled, then fell heavily, the camera striking the ground hard. Hamid drew her gently to her feet and she withheld a sob. She would *not* cry.

Pain she could handle. But if her Nikon was damaged in any way...

"You're with me now," he soothed. "Everything will be okay."

She nodded jerkily, then pulled out of his arms and scrambled for her camera. She cradled it in the palm of her hand, checking it over. Hamid would deal with the brigand now. She had her whole career on the line if her camera was broken.

Oomph.

She twisted around, her eyes widening at seeing the brigand and Hamid fighting. Though Hamid was clearly the better fighter as he ducked and weaved and threw punches, he was also no longer armed while the brigand wielded the same, big ugly blade he'd had pressed against her throat.

She couldn't risk Hamid getting stabbed and dying on her. A sob built at the base of her throat. A world without Hamid in it was like a world without an ocean.

It was reflex to stand with the camera's strap in her hand, then whirl with the camera flying around too before it hit the brigand with a *crack* against his temple, sending him unconscious to the ground.

She stood stunned and disbelieving at the parts of her camera that had flown free at the impact, her brain hardly able to compute what she'd done. As her precious camera fell from her grasp, Hamid was there, lifting her against his chest and taking her into the tent.

Chapter Ten

Holly couldn't help but stare up at Hamid as he laid her on the sleeping mat, and she was only vaguely aware of the other women scooting back out of the way. She probably looked like a drowned rat with her tangled red hair falling in a sodden mess down her back and her underwear barely covering her.

"You didn't need to do that," he said softly, tenderly.

"I couldn't let you die."

His smile was gentle, the very antithesis to how she'd imagined he'd act. "I was never at risk, my little flame. I'm well-versed in defeating my enemies." He took a shuddering breath. "That you put yourself at risk for me has me torn between fury and selfish glee."

She blinked. "You put yourself at risk for me, too."

He nodded. "I did. But I'm trained for combat. You're not."

"Because you're a sheikh and I'm a woman?" she asked bitterly.

His gaze hardened a little. "You don't like that I'm someone in power?"

She hated inequality of any type, most especially a man in power while a woman was considered powerless. Just like her parents. Her dad had always been the dominant figure, her mother yielding to him in every way.

She didn't get a chance to answer. One of the shrouded women touched Hamid on his arm. "I am happy to give you anything you desire." She turned to her friends. "We all are."

Hamid flinched and pulled his arm away. "Thank you, but I don't require any of your services. You are all free now to decide your own future. Leave with the man who made you submit to him, or accept a small offering to get you started again in a your new life, and I'll have my helicopter pick you up and take you home."

It was clear Stockholm syndrome was a real thing when only two of the six women stepped forward, the others wild-eyed and uncertain. But one-by-one they stepped forward and agreed to their new start.

One of Hamid's men stepped into the tent carrying a number of small cloth bags. He passed them to Hamid, who then pressed a bag into each of the hands of the women. "There is enough money inside each of these for you to restart your lives. If you get into trouble, there is also a number on a card you can contact."

The approaching *wak-wak-wak* of helicopter blades punctured the silence and the women appeared scared and grateful all at once as they were herded out by Hamid's man. A couple of the women babbled their gratitude and Hamid smiled and took it all in his stride.

Holly crossed her arms, ignoring the racket of the helicopter landing, and the sand that it blew against the tent. Only once the last woman had disappeared through the flap did Holly ask, "You've been able to communicate outside the desert all this time?" She despised how wobbly and hurt her voice sounded.

He nodded. "I have."

"Yet you never thought to tell me."

"You never asked."

"You knew I wanted to go home."

"Yet you're not following the women outside to climb into the helicopter with them."

"You'd allow me to leave?"

"Is that what you want?" he asked softly, his eyes holding hers.

She looked away, her mind filled with her camera that was smashed beyond repair. Her heart shriveled and her chest tightened as the back of her eyes burned. "I don't have a choice now. I'll have to return home and find some waitressing work or similar for a few years so that I can save for another camera and travel the world to take photos again."

The helicopter blades grew in volume once again as they twirled faster and faster. She didn't need to step outside to know the bird was even now lifting into the air with the women inside it. Even if she wanted to it was too late to leave.

Hamid's voice softened. "Or you could come home with me and I'll buy you a new camera."

She turned back to him. "Why would you do that?" She shook her head. "You said it yourself, you have women at home—"

She gaped. "Oh my god, you have a harem, don't you? But of course you do, you're a sheikh!"

He didn't deny it. "I don't care about those women. Not anymore. Once we're home they, too, will get a nice payout and I'll never have to see them again."

She blinked. "Why?"

"Isn't it obvious, little flame? I want to be with you." He exhaled roughly. "When I saw that desert savage holding a blade to your throat and I thought I might never see you again, never get the chance to—"

"To what, Hamid?" she asked softly.

He exhaled heavily. "To hold you in my arms again."

It was oddly deflating. But what had she expected? A marriage proposal? A declaration of love? She almost snorted. He was a sheikh. She was nobody. He might get rid of his pampered harem but the moment he got sick of Holly his harem would return or he'd create a new one. He'd probably even marry a sheikha one day soon and Holly would be cast off and never thought about again.

What do you care? It's not as if you want to settle down anytime soon and be stuck in a relationship for the rest of your life.

Her independence was everything to her. That and a successful career, which would see her continue to do what she loved: taking photos of her travels. A pity her camera was now in pieces and her career on the rocks.

You could always accept Hamid's suggestion.

The distant bleating of goats and bellow of camels grew louder as the brigands brought their thirsty animals to water. Holly sighed. The noise and commotion of the livestock would scare away any wildlife in the area.

She blinked at Hamid. "So...what would be expected of me if I agreed to be with you short term?"

His nostrils flared. "Who said anything about short term?"

"I need to travel to take photos. I can't do that in your palace."

"You'd be surprised how many photos you could take of my palace." At her frown he added, "I'm a private person. Photos there have been banned up to this point."

Adrenaline and excitement surged. "So you're saying I'd have free rein to take pictures of anything and anyone I wanted?"

He nodded. "On one condition."

"That being?"

"You stay with me for a month. After that if you want to leave, I won't stop you."

"That's blackmail!"

"It's logical. I believe we have something, little flame, and I want to explore it. You can walk away now, if that is what you want, or you can agree to my terms. It's your choice."

He put forward an amazing argument, one she couldn't say no to. A new camera and unlimited photos inside his palace with all her living expenses paid for. Not to mention spending glorious, lust-filled nights with him.

She exhaled softly, then nodded and said, "Agreed."

Chapter Eleven

Holly wandered through the palace, awestruck all over again. She might have been here now for two weeks but she was yet to get used to the extravagance of the gold-plated walls, the pools, fountains and unlimited water, and the mix of modern and antique furnishings that had to have cost millions.

That Hamid seemed so blasé about the whole thing, as though he could take it or leave it, left her in a constant state of amusement and despair.

She could never get used to such...excess. Not that she'd be here long enough to become familiar with the concept anyway. She'd photograph every square inch of the building, then she'd go on her merry way, where she'd take more magnificent shots of the rest of the world.

That her heart ached knowing she'd never see Hamid again was a bittersweet emotion she kept strictly in check. She'd enjoy these last two weeks with him and tuck their shared memories away for safekeeping. She'd never wanted a relationship or permanent ties and she wasn't about to start wishing for otherwise.

She stepped inside a huge ballroom with a black and white tiled floor. She gazed around, impressed by the sheer size of it. An arched dome with a mosaic glass skylight was centered above the huge dance floor. To one side a raised platform was where she guessed an orchestra would play and opposite that was an intimate, dark-stained wooden bar with a number of high-backed cane stools.

Her feet echoed eerily on the floor while workmen carried on with completing their work. Her nose wrinkled at the centuries old dust motes that floated in the beams of sunlight pouring through the skylight.

She'd heard work been done in the palace not even a week after she arrived, but she hadn't expected to find this ballroom. That it'd been transformed so quickly left her reeling. She should have been taking before and after photos!

She lifted her camera and took some snaps, amazed by how gorgeous the dancing motes looked under the colored skylights. If this ballroom was already gorgeous she could only imagine how beautiful it'd be once it was finished.

But she couldn't help but think it was way too pretentious for someone like Hamid. He wasn't the type to host ballroom parties let alone have one in his palace...was he?

It seemed the more she thought she knew Hamid, the less she really did. He was an enigma. Her desert rat rolled into sheikh all in one. That she was growing closer to him instead of farther apart had her acknowledging once again how she needed to protect her heart at all costs.

She stepped out of the ballroom and walked around the corner of yet another unexplored corridor when she thumped with an *oomph* into another woman. Holly stepped back and blinked at the gorgeous lady with long, ebony hair, her liquid dark eyes outlined in heavy kohl, and her slender yet curvaceous body barely hidden beneath a diaphanous silver gown that flowed over her like a waterfall.

Holly pressed a hand to her chest, the other holding her camera. "I'm terribly sorry. I didn't hear you coming." How could she have when the woman wore shoes that were more like ballet slippers that whispered as she walked?

The woman's eyes narrowed. "Do I know you?"

Holly blinked. She made it sound like Holly was an outsider, not an esteemed guest of Hamid's. "No, I don't think so. I've only been here a short time." She lifted her camera, the new one that Hamid had bought her. That he'd also managed to get her old one repaired had been a lovely, added bonus. "Is it okay if I take some photos of you?"

The other woman visibly relaxed. If she'd been a bird she would have preened. She most definitely wasn't shy. "Of course."

Holly lifted her camera. "Just act natural."

Click. Click. Click.

It could have been a real photo shoot. The other woman played up to the camera like a model. So unlike most of the women Holly had met inside the palace. The dark-haired beauty had no reservations. She was uninhibited and self-aware. She knew she was sexy and wasn't afraid to flaunt it.

Holly froze. *Holy shit.* Was this one of Hamid's women from the harem? She oozed sex appeal. But he'd told Holly he'd pay them out, hadn't he?

Her heart did a slow, painful somersault. Had she been too trusting, too naïve? She almost didn't blame Hamid for wanting this woman around. That Holly had never felt so plain and inadequate wasn't something she wanted to dwell on. She wasn't the jealous type.

"I see you've met my sister, Aisha."

She jumped at Hamid's voice behind her, then sagged as the truth slowly seeped into her pores. She should have known better. With their full lips, high cheekbones and brilliant eyes, there was a distinct family resemblance between Hamid and Aisha, their DNA seemingly drenched in sex appeal.

"So this is the woman everyone is talking about," Aisha giggled behind her hand.

Hamid glared at his sister. "What are you doing in those clothes?"

Aisha fluttered her eyelashes. "If they were fine for your lovers, then they must surely be fine for your little sister?"

"No, they're not. You're a sheikha, you need to dress like one."

Holly blinked. "This probably isn't any of my business, but shouldn't she be allowed to dress like she wants. Her body, her mind. Her rights."

Hamid twisted to Holly, his nostrils flared and lips tight. "This is the one time I don't want or need your western influence and ideals. My people don't expect the world from me, but they would never tolerate their sheikha dressing like this!"

He pushed a hand over his face and muttered, "I don't have time for this. I need to be someplace else." He looked at his sister and gritted, "Get changed." His stare lingered on Holly. "I'll see you both at dinner."

Holly nodded, and he seemed satisfied with that. He stalked off in his thobe, his dark plaits bouncing with every jerky step.

"Wow," Aisha murmured. "You must have really made an impression on him. He looked livid! He never reacts like that unless he cares." She smiled conspiratorially. "Are you also the reason he hasn't been drinking? It's been nice to see him sober."

Holly managed a smile in return. "He's been trying his best not to drink after learning I lived with a violent alcoholic father."

"So he *does* care about you." Her eyes sparkled, her mind apparently focused on the positive. "It's nice to know there is hope for him yet." She did a twirl, one hand holding out her gauzy material. "This isn't the only harem outfit that was left behind. Do you want to try some on?"

Holly smiled. "Do you think your brother would like seeing me in one of them?"

"Is the sky blue?" Aisha enquired sweetly. "That you're not his sister means you can wear whatever the hell you want." Her eyes tightened fractionally. "You are so lucky."

Holly managed to smile. "I am," she conceded. "As much as I adore your brother, freedom means everything to me."

Aisha blinked, her full lips twisting. "So many women would give up everything, including their freedom, just to be with him. You must be as strong as an oak resisting his charms compared to all those reeds bending to his every whim."

"An oak?" Holly snorted with laughter. "I'll take that as a compliment."

Aisha giggled. "You really are different, aren't you?"

Holly nodded. "I sure hope so."

Chapter Twelve

Holly looked in the mirror, feeling almost alien in the emerald harem outfit that fit her body perfectly, the color highlighting her unbound, red-gold hair and her sun-kissed skin. The diamond bodice flashed and twinkled under the lights, emphasizing the deep V of her cleavage. That the dress was all but backless, except for a strip across her ass, left her feeling risqué and excited.

Aisha touched the ends of Holly's hair. "So soft and gorgeous. The color reminds me of the desert. *Huh.* No wonder my brother is so hot for you." She waggled her fingers in front of her face like a fan. "If I didn't like men so much I might want you too."

Holly smiled. "For someone so stunning you sure know how to flatter."

"I'm only being truthful."

Holly's cheek tinged with pink. "Thank you. I wish I could say I take after my mother. But it's my father who had the red hair. Unfortunately he also had the red-hot temper to go along with it."

Aisha's lips thinned. "Your father sounds like an asshole. Luckily you only inherited the color of his hair." She threw a long, silken wrap around Holly's barely there outfit, then grabbed hold of Holly's nearest hand. "Come, let's go surprise my brother."

Holly picked up her camera with a laugh, and followed Aisha through half-a-dozen corridors where paintings and sculptures beckoned along the way, along with priceless vases and colorful urns.

She took little notice of where they were going until Aisha opened a door and they stepped inside an interview room, where Hamid sat behind a desk while speaking to reporters and journalists.

Holly paused inside the doorway, her eyes glued to the man who made her pulse race and her throat dry. That he was freshly shaven and in a western suit, but with his overlong hair still plaited, somehow made her want him more. If he was her fantasy brought to life in his thobe, he was a double shot of deliciousness in the dark gray suit that clung to his hardness, a white dress shirt contrasting against his dark-golden skin.

She leaned close to Aisha. "Seems like he's a little busy right now," she whispered.

"He'll be done soon enough," Aisha promised with a little smirk. "Come on."

Hamid chose that moment to lift his eyes, his stare widening as he caught sight of Holly. His lips curled and his eyes flashed at seeing her outfit, and Holly felt a stirring deep inside, an answering sexual need she just barely repressed.

"Oh my," Aisha murmured. "And he hasn't even seen your outfit properly yet."

One of the reporters lifted a hand, and Hamid nodded vaguely at him while not once looking away from Holly.

"So what *are* you doing exactly to help save Imbranak's wildlife from extinction?"

Hamid finally unlocked his stare from Holly to focus on the reporter. "As I said, I have men in the desert recording any sightings and observing the activity of the animals in the territory. Those same men are also tasked to protect the wildlife from humans who might hunt or kill them."

"So your desert wildlife charity continues to save many of these animals?"

"Of course. The desert is a harsh environment. But our native animals have adapted and sometimes even thrived as long as mankind stays clear."

Holly pressed a hand to her mouth. It was all starting to make so much sense now. Hamid not only loved the desert, he loved the creatures in it too. Little wonder he knew what animals visited the oasis and when. There was a purpose for his escape to the sandy wilderness. That it wasn't just for his own sanity made him even more charismatic in her eyes.

"So you have proof then that there are still Arabian leopards in the wild?"

Hamid smiled and nodded, then swept a hand toward the blank wall behind him, where a projector proceeded to light up a photo of the one and same big cat that Holly had snapped near the oasis. "I was lucky enough to procure an amazing photographer who took this shot and many, many more."

He paused, his gaze moving around the room for dramatic effect. His audience appeared to hang onto his every word. He smiled magnanimously. "That same photographer will be showcasing an exhibition of her work, here inside my palace, very soon."

Holly's stomach bottomed out while she trembled between desperate hope and bitter denial. Why hadn't he run this idea past her first? Did he think she needed his name to make her famous?

Was he damn well right?

The news generated a babble of excited mutterings and as Hamid's gaze moved back towards her, every stare of every reporter in the room landed on her, the apparent star-in-the-making.

Hamid smiled encouragement, then stood as he announced, "And here is the photographer herself. Everyone, I'd like you to meet Holly Petersen."

She was nothing short of a deer in headlights. Made worse when she realized Aisha had slipped out of the room, leaving her to fend for herself. No doubt the sister of a sheikh didn't want any bad publicity while she was in a harem outfit.

Too bad Holly's outfit was even more revealing. She only hoped the wrap concealed more than it exposed because, right then, she had no one but herself to rely on. But then she'd grown up being self-sufficient. She'd had no choice.

Fake it till you make it.

Holly managed to paste on a confident smile as she sashayed farther into the room, feeling half-naked with so many eyes on her. "Thank you Sheikh Hamid, you are too kind."

Hamid winked. "And you are far too modest."

She couldn't think about her daring harem outfit. It was enough that she brazened her way through this confrontation without leaving her name and profession in tatters by a bunch of overzealous reporters.

One of them with a big, bulbous nose and black-peppered-with-gray beard pushed a microphone close to her face. "Can you tell us about the upcoming exhibition? What photos will you showcase? Will those same photos be available to purchase?"

She cleared her throat. "I've taken hundreds of wildlife photos, the best of which will be available to buy. I've also taken some very impressive photos of Sheikh Hamid. He is quite the photogenic subject."

A female reporter stepped forward, her dove-gray hijab perfectly in place. "Are they available for purchase, too?"

Holly looked at Hamid, sensing his scowl even though he smiled and said, "Those ones will be...negotiable."

"Out of my price range then, clearly," the female reporter said with a dramatic little sigh. She looked Holly up and down, a feral gleam in her dark brown eyes. "So tell us, *Holly,* is what you have on now also what you'd wear while photographing animals in the desert?"

Holly glanced down at her thin, silk wrap. It was a little too translucent for her liking. "Of course not. Most of the time I wore one of Hamid's thobes. I found them particularly comfortable while lying on the sand."

Hamid smirked at her little tidbit of information, as though pleased by her honesty. The reporters went ballistic.

A young man pushed past the female reporter and asked in an excited, nasally voice, "Are you and Sheikh Hamid dating?"

Holly's throat closed. *Holy shit.* This wasn't going well. She didn't even know if what she had with Hamid *was* a relationship. She bit her bottom lip, her mind coming up blank.

She sensed Hamid behind her even before he stepped close and put a proprietary arm around her waist, lending her strength. Yet seeing his eyes shining with tenderness as he looked down at her sent her knees weak and her pulse surging.

"There is probably little use in hiding the truth any longer, little flame." He tore his gaze away from her and back to their spellbound audience. "Holly and I *are* exclusive."

Chapter Thirteen

Holly was used to being the photographer, not the one in front of the camera. Lights flashed and fizzed even as Hamid led her from the room and said, "This interview is over."

The young reporter almost stumbled into them in his eagerness to get in the last word. "Sheikh Hamid, when is this exhibition?"

Holly frowned. Shouldn't the reporter be asking her that question since she was the one supposedly holding the exhibition?

Hamid paused, then turned to face the crowd of reporters, journalists and cameramen. "It will be held this Friday in the recently built ballroom. Invitations will be sent out tomorrow."

Hamid twisted away to pull open a door and draw her through it. He shut it behind them, and she was only vaguely aware of a big oak desk with a computer, of the musty scent of aged, leather bound books inside their shelves as she looked up at him. Her stomach fluttered and her heart was fit to burst through her chest. But if she was expecting an explanation she couldn't have been more wrong.

He pushed her back against the door as he bent and his mouth crashed onto hers. That a crowd of nosy reporters might still be on the other side of the doorway quickly faded into obscurity.

Nothing mattered but the hot, demanding pressure of his lips on hers, the hard, adept touch of his calloused hands as they slipped under her wrap to the skimpy outfit beneath, caressing the shape of her, tracing every dip and line while goosebumps flared over her skin.

He pushed her hair aside and kissed the vulnerable side of her throat. Sensation poured through her like a tsunami. God, she was drowning in his skilled lovemaking, lost to him—

He pulled back, his glittering eyes full of need and a whole lot of pent-up desire. "Take off your wrap."

"Wh-what?" She was too dazed to comprehend anything outside the sphere of lust surrounding her.

"I've been aching to see exactly what you're wearing."

The heat inside her skyrocketed to scorching, her hands shaking as she pushed off her wrap and bared her outfit beneath.

But then a sudden tide of self-doubt hit her. She was in a harem outfit, but she was no harem girl. She was Holly fricking Petersen. She didn't do sexy.

Except all doubts lifted like mist on a baking hot day as his eyes darkened and a muscle ticked to life in his jaw, not to mention the massive erection he sported inside his pants. "I love it."

"I love your suit, too," she admitted.

There was something unreservedly hot and decadent about seeing him in the finest tailored western clothes, the suit highlighting his wealthy sheikh status while reminding her of the man beneath...the desert rat who knew exactly how to turn her on.

"Dance for me," he said hoarsely.

She could no more disobey his request that a bee could deny its instinct to collect pollen. She wanted him to always remember her, wanted him to think about her as much as she knew she'd think about him.

He took a step back to give her space and she lifted her arms above her head and swiveled her hips from side-to-side. She didn't need music. The beat was their shared pulse that synchronized them as one, a silent harmony that allowed her to shimmy and sway.

The tiny priceless diamonds on the bodice twinkled and shook, the barely there skirt with its train at the back swishing with every movement. "Am I a good little harem girl?" she asked with a flutter of her eyelashes.

His stare blazed with need. "If you'd been a part of my harem I would never have let you go."

She smiled, empowered by his words. She might have been a small, powerless girl quivering with fear and uncertainty when her parents had fought, but right now she quivered with a far different emotion.

"You're a goddess," he said huskily. "One I want to worship."

There was no more dancing necessary, except the gyrating against his tongue once he'd undressed her and he knelt at her feet with his head between her thighs. His first few licks sent heat straight to her core. The next dozen left her weak and helpless against the door. The finale sent starbursts fizzing and exploding behind her eyelids.

She was still dazed and mindless with pleasure when he pushed to his feet, released his cock from the zipper of his pants, slid on a condom from the pocket of his pants, then lifted her high, one-handing his shaft to guide it to her center.

She gasped at his entry, caught between pleasure and pain even as she was vaguely aware of the muttering of voices behind the door. The reporters were still there?

The knowledge sent her inner heat factor to a whole new level of inferno. And as Hamid began stroking inside her, his hand had to cover her mouth and muffle her cries of ecstasy as he filled her, pushing in and out, faster and faster, his strokes hitting a spot that sent her tumbling headfast into an abyss of pleasure so intense she lost her voice, her scream all on the inside.

Hamid's eyes rolled back as he too succumbed to ecstasy, his whole body convulsing as he emptied his seed. It seemed like forever before they both got their breath back, her legs still wrapped around Hamid's hips as he leaned his head against hers.

"Incredible," he said hoarsely.

She couldn't have agreed more.

"Do you think anyone heard us?"

"I'm not sure."

"If they did, let's hope they didn't record it."

Hamid chuckled. "If they're smart they would have done exactly that. The press knows I'd pay big money to have it deleted and our privacy intact." He shifted his head a little so that his mouth grazed hers, his kiss tender. "But for now we should probably get dressed and get out of here before someone comes sniffing around."

She withheld a shuddery sigh when he drew away and disposed of the condom. That she was emotionally empty at the physical disconnect left her a little shaken. She'd be gone soon; she couldn't afford this emotional attachment to him.

"Are you okay?" he asked huskily.

She nodded and forced a smile as she dressed. "It's not my first rodeo."

He pulled his zipper up with a snort, his eyes darkening as she slid the dress back over her head. "It should be illegal for you to dress like that."

"Have you checked yourself in the mirror lately?"

He cocked his head to one side. "So you really do like me in a suit?"

"I adore you in a suit."

He clasped her hand and led her out of what was probably his office and into yet another wide corridor, his grin cocky. "Then I'll be sure to wear one more often."

She glanced up at him, her mind already whirring. "Did you really mean what you said to those reporters about an exhibition?"

"Of course. I don't say anything I don't mean."

"That only gives me three days to prepare everything."

"Don't stress about it. I've already put together a team for you to work with."

"You have?" she squeaked. "But of course you have."

He slanted a look at her. "You don't sound impressed."

"I'm an independent woman, Hamid, I've made it on my own so far without—"

"Without my help, I get it," he said astutely. "And you don't want me to steamroll you with my money and my contacts."

She nodded. "Don't get me wrong, I'm grateful, I really am. And I'm not going to say no to an exhibition now that you've organized one for me."

He sent her a wary look. "But you would have preferred that I discussed it with you first?"

She nodded. "Yes."

He exhaled. "I'll be sure to remember that for next time."

She smiled sadly. "We have two more weeks together. There probably won't be a next time."

His eyes darkened, his hand that clasped hers tightening. "You know nothing would please me more than if you stayed longer."

Her heart ached at the thought even as she shook her head. "We both know that's not going to happen." At his clenched jaw she added softly, "I don't want to sound ungrateful. You *did* save my life."

"Don't hold that against me," he said drily.

"I just want to enjoy what's left of our time together. I'm a free spirit, Hamid, just like you. It's probably what drew us together in the first place."

"You would feel trapped here with me?"

"I honestly don't know." She managed a smile, once again aware just how much she'd miss him. And therein lay the problem. She *needed* to leave before she had no resistance left against him.

Chapter Fourteen

Holly woke to Hamid's lips covering hers, and a shaft of sunlight dazzling behind her eyelids. She smiled and forced open her eyes, noting his taut, naked body over hers, his erection digging into her body. She stretched. "Mm. I could get used to this."

He grinned, then drew back. "Sorry, my insatiable little flame, but as much as I'd clearly love some late morning sex, there's no time. We both overslept and now the helicopter is waiting for us."

She blinked, her mind whirling. "Wait. What? Are we meant to be going somewhere?"

He nodded. "Yes, but it's a surprise."

He climbed off her, his buttocks deliciously rounded and paler than the long length of his tanned back that flexed and rippled with every movement. God, he could have been an athlete. Then he stalked into the walk-in closet to get dressed, calling out, "You might want to hurry. And don't forget your camera."

That was enough for her to jerk out of bed. "I'm taking photos?"

"Yes, that's the general idea." He stalked back out in his thobe and sandals, his clever hands making quick work of some plaits in his hair. "I've arranged a picnic basket so we can enjoy a late lunch once we land."

Her stomach gurgled. She was already hungry, but it wouldn't hurt her to miss breakfast just once. "Will there be people where we're going? What do I wear?"

"Dress for the desert," he said simply. "Sunscreen, a hat and long sleeves."

Fifteen minutes later she was climbing into the helicopter with him and gazing with delight out at the palace as they rose into the air. The huge building shimmered under the midday sun, the twin turrets of its rooftop then disappearing beneath them as the helicopter veered away sharply to reveal an endless expanse of desert and not much else.

When they finally landed once again, it was back at the oasis where at least half of his men had remained along with all the camels. She smiled as Essam half-ran toward them while bent over, clutching at his headgear so that the force of the spinning rotors didn't tear it off his head.

He opened the door and Hamid nodded at him as he climbed out with the picnic basket in one hand before he turned to offer Holly his other hand. She accepted it, then ducked and laughed as they raced out of the swirling particles of sand stirred up by the rotors. Only once they were safely inside Hamid's tent did the helicopter lift into the air again and disappear.

Essam bent his head. "Sheikh Hamid. Holly. It's good to see you both again."

Holly smiled and Hamid nodded and said, "You too, Essam."

"Everything has been prepared, as requested, with Camille saddled up and ready to go."

Hamid nodded. "No sign of the brigands?"

"No, I doubt we'll ever see them again. And it's unlikely any more brigands are around, not knowing those ones we dispatched were ruling this part of the desert."

Holly pressed a hand to her chest, her heart stuttering erratically. She'd had a couple of nightmares about the man with the blade at her throat, her psyche not yet over the ordeal. That she'd been brought up in a violent environment seemed only to have underscored her deep-seated fears.

"You'll be fine," Hamid said, his shrewd eyes reading her distress. "I'll kill anyone who tries to hurt you."

"I don't doubt that for a second," she said in a shaky voice, then laughed a little off-note as she added, "I can't believe I'm saying this, but I'm looking forward to this camel ride." Her eyes widened as comprehension dawned. "We're going to that same place you promised to take me before the brigands attacked us, aren't we?"

Hamid smiled, but his eyes were still sharp and assessing at her change of subject. "We are." Placing her camera so that it was nestled in a rug inside the picnic basket, he drew her with him from their tent toward Camille. The camel was kneeling on the sand already saddled and bridled. "I never make promises I can't keep, and this way you'll get some more photos for your exhibition."

She smiled, but a different kind of anxiety now pinched at her innards. She had so much yet to do. Choosing and printing her photos, deciding which ones to make glossy or matte, panoramic or square, black and white or color, and which ones to frame. Then there was the task of hanging them and lighting them.

The work ahead was endless and yet here she was going on a mini-working holiday with her lover.

Their mount bellowed when she saw Hamid, her blinking, long-lashed eyes and hoarse welcome making Hamid chuckle. "You missed me, didn't you Camille?"

Holly grinned. How had she ever imagined her lover was anything but a gentleman? Oh, he had his violent side; she'd witnessed it firsthand when he'd protected her from the desert brigands. She also had a feeling he'd be ruthless if needed for his country.

What about when he drinks?

She shivered, but managed to ignore the little voice inside her head. He'd stopped drinking for her and that was good enough until or unless he proved otherwise. She couldn't control him. She could only trust in him.

She climbed behind Hamid and wrapped her arms around his waist, enjoying his corded strength. She was far more comfortable and confident now as Camille rocked into a standing position, and it was relief when she and Hamid didn't bang heads. How he balanced the picnic basket in front of him though, she had no idea.

She stayed calm until the moment Hamid commanded their camel into a gallop that ate up the ground, the oasis and camp soon far behind them and nothing but sand and dunes to be seen.

Camille seemed comfortable in her stride, and Holly let loose with a joyous *hoot* as adrenaline and excitement pumped through her. That the sand blurred either side of them made her realize how fast their mount was traveling. Hamid laughed as he slowed Camille, bringing her from a rocking gallop into a bone-jarring trot and finally a long, bouncy walk.

He looked back at her and winked, "Enjoying the ride?"

She snorted and said saucily, "I'm certain I'd enjoy riding something else—*someone* else—a whole lot more."

His body stiffened as his voice pitched low. "I'm going to hold you to that, little flame."

She grinned at his promise as much as she did at hearing his endearment. That there was also a feral need clamoring for release within only highlighted how perfectly suited they were to one another. She cleared her throat and conceded, "At least now I understand why you enjoy getting away to the desert, riding your camel and swimming in the oasis in seclusion."

"You and I aren't so different. You crave those quiet moments too. Your career reflects that every time you photograph a sunset or sunrise, every time you stay poised with your camera for hours waiting for wildlife."

He was right. Even when she was in a crowd taking photos of all the diverse people it was nothing short of a relief to return to those quiet moments, kneeling or lying on her stomach in a marsh or sand, sometimes in water or mud, taking shots of whatever Mother Nature delivered.

She adjusted her floppy straw hat, glad she'd also decided to wear a traditional abaya over her leggings and T-shirt. That and her hat would help to keep her skin from burning, and the abaya was about as comfortable as clothes got. Even her ankle boots were perfect for the camel ride.

So different to her last time on a camel.

She grinned. That the abaya was a colorful rainbow of colors meant it wasn't really traditional—black was the favored color—but it suited her style perfectly.

Pressing closer to him, her breasts mashing against his back, she ran her hands up and down his torso. "I'm impatient to know where you're taking me."

"You'll see very soon," he said hoarsely.

She pressed the side of her face to his back, careless of the hat's rim folding over. There was something so right in absorbing Hamid's body heat and hearing the strong tattoo of his heartbeat.

She sighed. It was going to break her leaving him, but it'd break her even more if she stayed. If there was one lesson she'd learned from her childhood, it was that no man was worth the sacrifice of sticking around. Her future lay elsewhere. She'd had her life mapped out for as long as she could remember. Travel the world taking photos, and make a career out of it.

The desert landscape soon changed, the sand softening under Camille's hooves, the scattering of rocks that appeared here and there soon becoming a carpet of them with a few boulders standing tall and ancient from out of the sand.

Hamid stopped Camille beside a couple of straggly ghaf trees, which provided a little bit of welcome shade. The camel dropped to her knees, and Holly again swung with the motion.

"Can I ask what's here?" she asked softly.

"A sand cat lives in a burrow he made in the soft sand over there next to some rocks," he murmured. "We've been keeping an eye on him for six months now. Unlike most nocturnal hunting cats, he seems to prefer hunting mid-afternoon."

They dismounted and Holly's mind was already imagining the shots she'd get of the animal. Hamid took hold of the picnic basket in one hand and clasped her hand in his other, leading her toward another shadier tree. Opening the picnic basket, he handed the camera to her, then took out a rug and laid it out onto the ground.

They lay down on their bellies, side-by-side, their gazes locked on the not too distant burrow. But though the merciless sun was past its zenith, nothing with a heartbeat was moving. It was far too hot.

They lay still for what had to be an hour when Hamid rolled toward her and murmured, "Looks like we're out of luck."

She sighed and nodded, then turned onto her back and lifted her camera. "How about a selfie of us both?"

He chuckled, and stretched out onto his back next to her, his arms behind his head. "Sure."

She was laughing with him when she clicked a shot of them, then put her camera aside and climbed onto him. Looking down at him, his smile becoming dark, heated, she said huskily, "I believe I mentioned something about riding a certain someone."

Chapter Fifteen

Holly popped a juicy date into her mouth and sighed luxuriously. It was wonderful to be naked, and though she couldn't stay that way for much longer for fear of sunburn—even in the mid-afternoon shade she'd be burned to a crisp—she'd enjoy it while she could. "I can't eat one more crumb."

"You *did* nearly eat the entire contents of the picnic bastard, not including the blanket and camera," he said drily, amusement glinting in his gaze.

He pushed onto his elbow on his side and leaned down to kiss her. They might have made love half-an-hour or so ago, but it didn't stop her from enjoying the seductive press of his lips on hers, the touch of his satiny, naked skin under her hands, and the power he wielded so effortlessly over her.

He stiffened, his head lifting and his eyes fixed on a point behind her head.

Her heart raced and her adrenaline spiked, while her voice came out shrill. "What is it?"

He smiled. "You might want your camera now."

It was pure reflex to reach for her Nikon, roll onto her stomach then focus on the desert cat as its head peered above its burrow, its nose twitching and its oversized ears flickering.

She knew enough about the cats to know they were incredible predators. They managed to get most of their fluids from their prey, existing without water for much of their lives.

It suddenly shot out of its burrow, its huge, fluffy paws not even making a mark on the sand as it crouched low and moved forward, clearly on a mission. It wasn't until she took some shots of the animal that she realized exactly what that mission was.

A yellowy-brown, striped snake slithered slowly across the sand in the shade of the rocks and trees, its tongue flickering and its head raised a little.

Holly's whole body tensed as the cat attacked. It struck at the snake with its paws, its sharp claws digging deep before it jumped back as the snake went to strike. It was like a well-choreographed dance with the cat batting at the snake's head or body a nanosecond before it tried to strike.

In the end the cat was too agile, its claws too sharp, and the snake succumbed to its injuries. The desert cat trotted back to its burrow with its head high and the snake in its mouth, the snake's tail trailing behind in the sand.

"Oh wow, that was intense!" she enthused.

He grinned. "Was it? I must have been too busy enjoying my naked lover in her element taking photos."

Her face burned a little, and she cursed her pale skin that flushed so easily. "I'm glad you weren't too bored."

She put down her camera and moved closer to him, his arm pillowing her head. She smiled. How was she so comfortable with this man? Anyone else would be bowing and scraping to him, respecting their sheikh. She was as natural around him as a woman could be with any lover.

Her lashes fluttered closed and tiredness pulled at her. The heat, the excitement and the energy she'd used making love had clearly taken their toll. A smile pulling at her lips, all thoughts faded as she succumbed to sleep.

She woke in the single bed at her parent's house, the sounds of an argument causing her stomach to fill with dread. *Not again.* She climbed out of bed, her bare feet touching the cool linoleum floor. She shivered, wishing only to be safe and warm, and cocooned from the nightmare that was her life.

Her dad's voice thundered through the walls. "You're not wearing that to the shops. What are you, a whore?"

Her mother's soft voice barely registered. "But it's just a singlet. I-I've worn it before and you didn't care."

Crack.

Her mother didn't cry out, didn't say one more word in self-defense. Of course she didn't. She'd learned the hard way it only made things worse. Better to submit and act docile than rebel and earn more hits.

The same couldn't be said for Holly. Something unraveled inside her, a dark fury set off its leash. She marched toward her tall wicker basket with its sports paraphernalia inside, and grabbed her baseball bat. Jerking open her bedroom door, she stepped into the lounge room. Her father was bent over her mom, who lay in a fetal position on the floor.

"Leave her alone," Holly growled. She wielded her bat in the air as she approached. "Or feel what it's like to be beaten black-and-blue."

Her father straightened slowly, and twisted to face her, his eyes narrowing and his lips curling into a feral smirk. "You wouldn't have the guts, girl."

"Try me," she gritted.

He stood still for a long minute, then exhaled heavily. "She's not worth it. Neither one of you are worth it."

He spun on his heel and pushed open the front door. Then turning back to them, he announced, "Just make sure the groceries are done before I'm home again."

Then he was gone.

Holly didn't bother to tell him to go fuck himself. She was just glad the danger was behind them until the next time. She dropped the bat onto the floor and raced toward her mom, unprepared for the sight of her bloodied and broken nose, the purplish-black bruise and swollen eye.

"Oh my god, Mom. We need to get you to a hospital."

Her mom shook her graying head. "No, no. *No!* They'll ask questions that I can't tell them—"

"Like *what,* Mom? That your husband uses you as a punching bag and you're terrified of him. Maybe it's time you told them the truth and found a way to escape from his violence."

Her mom's whole body tensed, her face paler than ever. "He'll beat me up, maybe even kill me if I say a word against him. I-I can't risk that. Not for anything."

Holly's heart sank. "Not even for me?"

The dream faded as cool air brushed over her skin. She opened her eyes to find Hamid awake and fully dressed as he watched her.

"You were dreaming," he said softly.

She swallowed past her dry throat. "Wh-what did I say?"

"Nothing I could understand. Your body was twitching and you muttered some incomprehensible words."

She exhaled softly. "Good."

He arched a brow. "You know, you can trust me to share your personal demons. I'm here for you, little flame.'

"Thank you. That means a lot."

"But you're not ready right now?" he said tonelessly.

"Not yet, but maybe one day." By which time she'd be far, far away.

She sat and her abaya, which he must have put over her while she was asleep to protect her from sunburn, slipped back off. Suddenly aware of her nakedness, his flared eyes and hissed breath made her ten times more self-conscious and she became Miss Fumble-Fingers as she dressed in her clothes.

She glanced at Hamid and he managed a smile and said, "No need to cover up on my account. You're gorgeous."

She paused, his intensity half-thrilling, half-terrifying. Their connection was beginning to feel all too real. A buzzing awareness went through her. This could be her forever if she wanted it, if they *both* wanted it. Yearning tore through her, leaving her reeling.

What the actual fuck?

She didn't want to feel like this...she didn't want this, period. She was a free spirit who wasn't bogged down by emotional ties and commitments. She didn't want a permanent relationship.

Are you sure about that?

Of course!

"Are you okay?" he asked gently.

She nodded as she pulled on her leggings and boots. "Yes, I'm fine." She managed a smile in return. "Thank you for bringing me here. I took some awesome shots of the desert cat. Not to mention that poor snake."

"You're welcome. And that's life in the desert. Opportunistic hunting is the only way to survive out here."

The sun was dipping low on the horizon by the time they finally mounted and rode back to camp. The helicopter streaked over them as they were riding into camp, the *womp womp womp* of its rotors upsetting Camille enough to make her bellow.

"Good timing," Holly said.

Hamid leaned forward and stroked Camille's neck. "The pilot knew to return at dusk."

"We're not staying tonight?"

"Did you want to?"

"In a way, yes. But I also want to go through my photos and make a start on which ones to use."

He nodded. "I thought so. You'll get to meet your team tomorrow, too. You won't have to stress too much about anything with them there."

"Thank you."

For once she was relieved and grateful not to be completely independent and alone. Having others help would loosen the load and maybe she'd even learn something from them. Photography was one thing, exhibitions were quite another.

This opportunity might have fallen into her lap thanks to her affair with a sheikh, but she was no longer willing to cut off her nose to spite her face. Being independent was well and good, but she accepted now that refusing an offer to further her career was beyond silly.

She'd be thankful for her windfall that might well propel her into becoming a sought after photographer.

After dismounting and giving Camille a well-deserved pat, Hamid grabbed their picnic basket with her precious camera inside, then clasped Holly's hand in his free one as they walked toward the helicopter. She lifted a hand to the men who remained at the desert camp. Qaahir was noticeably absent, but then he was probably cooking up a storm back at the palace now Hamid had returned there.

She bet the men missed the talented chef.

It wasn't until she was settled and harnessed into her seat that the helicopter launched into the air, and she realized her own life had taken off too. And it was all thanks to Hamid.

Chapter Sixteen

Holly all but floated around her exhibition held inside the ballroom, grateful for Hamid's support as she held onto his proprietorial arm. That the room was overflowing with esteemed guests in their jewels and fancy clothes only added to the overall impression of achievement and success.

That she was with the most handsome man in the room, his black suit impeccable and his scent of citrus and frankincense leaving her close to swooning added dramatically to the positive vibes.

"You're stunning," Hamid murmured.

She looked down at her gown that was a tasteful mix between an abaya and an evening dress, the sparkling white silk draping to the floor and cinched at the waist by a gold belt. She'd forgone jewelry, her one concession being the jeweled clip that held her hair up in an elaborate topknot, some strands falling free to frame her face.

"Thank you." She smiled up at him. Even in her gold heels she was shorter than him by a few good inches. "I don't need to tell you that you're gorgeous."

"As long as you think so that's all I care about."

A man in a thobe approached them and bowed his head. "Sheikh Hamid, so sorry to disturb you at this inopportune time, but you have an urgent phone call to attend."

Hamid's lips thinned a little before he turned to Holly. "Will you excuse me for a moment? I do hate to leave you on your big night."

She quashed down disappointment. As sheikh he was a busy man, she needed to accept that. "I'll be fine, honestly. The sooner you go the sooner I can have you back."

Hamid bent and kissed her gently on the lips, then brushed his mouth along her ear and said, "I won't be long."

She shivered delicately, a cascade of goose bumps rippling over her arms even as Hamid disappeared from the ballroom and his sister entered it.

Aisha swept inside dressed in a classy hijab with gems embedded into the neckline, hem and cuffs of her turquoise outfit. Her glossy black hair was pulled back into a single braid with tiny flowers woven through it, her face lightly made-up with kohl, nude lipstick and mascara.

"You made it," Holly said with a smile.

"Of course, I wouldn't have missed this for the world. A shame my brother looks to have been pulled into yet another crisis."

Holly's smile diminished. "Yes, but he shouldn't be long."

"Is that what he told you?" Aisha said with a shake of her head. "I'll be surprised if he makes it back within the hour." Her eyes widened as she scanned the photos affixed to temporary cubicle walls. "Wow, you really are talented, aren't you?"

"Thank you. Though it's as much about the lighting and placement as it is about the photos."

Aisha arched a brow. "You're also very modest."

"I might have taken the photos but it was a team effort putting this all together. Hamid really did give me a great crew to showcase these photos."

"If there's one thing my brother does well, it's surrounding himself with the right people to get things done." She inhaled sharply and blinked, her expression turning serious, almost predatory as she spotted a tall man across the room. "Well good luck," she said vaguely, "I have someone I need to catch up with."

Holly nodded, trying not to gawp at the stranger who'd captured Aisha's attention. At first glimpse the man was obviously older with his dark hair peppered with gray. His suit of finest quality also revealed his wealth. "Sure. I'll see you soon."

Holly accepted a glass of champagne from a waiter who was circulating the room. She plastered a smile on her face as she thanked strangers who stopped her to congratulate and praise her on the various photographs.

Without conceit the photos really were good. She'd captured a moment in time that she hoped someone else would appreciate even half as much as she did. She walked around the ballroom, taking in some of her favorite shots.

The gorgeous sunset at the oasis, the camels' reflections shimmering black in the orange tinted water. The sand cat poised mid-attack with its legs outstretched and razor sharp claws unsheathed, the snake hooded and tall in defense. The hostile brigands charging toward Hamid as he stood motionless to fire a warning shot. The leopard lapping at the water. And the calm of the oasis in the valley below, the water a sparkling blue and the date palms a vivid green.

She didn't stop until she was in front of one of the two selfies she'd taken of Hamid and herself. She usually cringed at her own photos but there had been something irresistible at seeing the pure joy and intimacy radiating from them both as they smiled into the camera.

"I guess you think you're really something now, huh?"

Holly glanced at the woman who'd appeared from out of nowhere. There was no denying the woman's exquisite beauty, from her flashing brown eyes and bleached blonde hair, to the diamond in her aquiline nose and the sequined dress that fit her toned body like a second skin. "Excuse me?"

"Sheikh Hamid was mine until you came along and ruined everything." Her eyes shot daggers. "He'll get sick of you, too, you know. He does with all his women."

Holly's stomach knotted. "Let me guess, you were one of the women in his harem."

The woman's face twisted. "Not just any woman. I was his favorite. He—"

"Ranna, it's time for you to leave before you cause a scene. I have no doubt Hamid would banish you from Imbranak just for showing up here."

Ranna's hands fisted at her sides, her eyes blazing. "*She* is the intruder, not me!" she hissed, before she whirled around and pushed through the throng of people. No doubt escaping before suffering any repercussions.

"I'm sorry about Ranna," the man said smoothly. His charcoal designer suit fitted his tall, lean body perfectly. "Hamid will be livid when he finds out she was here." He smiled, his teeth white against his golden skin. "I'm Dhamar. Hamid is a close friend of my brother's—Sheikh Jamal. Unfortunately Jamal couldn't get here so I came in his place."

Holly's heart was still beating erratically from the confrontation with Ranna. She took in some calming breaths. It was bad enough that her stomach burned knowing they had been lovers. She couldn't allow it to spoil her big night. "I'm Holly. It's lovely to meet you, Dhamar."

"Believe me, the pleasure is all mine." He turned to admire the selfie. "Out of all the photos, this one is my favorite. I've never seen Hamid so openly filled with joy." He chuckled. "I most definitely never thought I'd see the day he'd leave single life and partying behind to fall in love and marry."

"Marry?" It was Holly's turn to laugh. "That is never going to happen. Hamid and I have an understanding. I have one more week here then I'm leaving."

Dhamar raised a brow. "I mightn't be one of his closest friends, but I know of his bet. He wouldn't have commissioned someone to build this ballroom if he wasn't serious about you. He intends to make you his wife."

"Wh-what?" Her heart thumped harder than ever, as much with hope as it did with doubt. "That's ridiculous. I might be his lover but he's still a bachelor and I have no doubt he'll remain one for a long time yet to come."

"So you're not planning on sticking around?" Dhamar asked, his eyes losing some of their warmth.

"Of course not." Ranna's words rang in her ears. *He'll get sick of you, too, you know. He does with all his women.* Holly dragged in a steadying breath. "Thanks to Hamid, I'll be leaving on a high note. There's nothing to keep me here anymore.'"

Liar. You'd stay if he professed his love for you.

The back of her neck prickled. She turned, instinctively knowing it was Hamid even before she saw his white face and dark, wounded eyes.

"Hamid," she breathed. "I don't know what you heard, but I didn't mean—"

"I heard everything," he said hoarsely. "And we both know you meant every word." He spun away and disappeared around a cubicle wall that displayed half a dozen more of her blown-up photographs.

"Shit."

Dhamar's face softened. By your reaction I take it you *do* care for him."

She bit her bottom lip, and nodded. "Yes, I guess I do." She pressed a hand to her brow. "I *know* I do." She cleared her throat, then added, "Thank you for stepping in earlier and saving the day."

"You're welcome." He tilted his dark head to the side. "But it seems to me you have a heartbroken man to chase down. Don't let his reputation fool you, Holly. He's a good guy." He nodded toward the selfie photo. "And you clearly make him happy. I'd hate to see him go back to the womanizing, borderline alcoholic he was becoming before he met you."

Chapter Seventeen

Hamid had no conscious thought of where he was going until the moment he arrived at the ballroom's bar. He sank onto a stool, his mind splintering right along with his heart.

"A shot of vodka," he said to the barman. "Actually, make it a dozen. Line them up." Was any amount of liquor going to numb the jagged pain of Holly's words? Right then he was willing to give it a try.

He was pleasantly light-headed and well on the way to being numb when he sensed Holly approaching.

"You're drinking." She sighed. "I looked everywhere in the ballroom but here. I really am naïve, aren't I?"

"You're many things, but naïve isn't one of them," he bit out.

She'd told Dhamar there wasn't anything to keep her here anymore. Her goal was clearly done. Hamid had given her the fame she craved, and along with it all the money she could want via her photography skills.

You could give her so much more. But are you willing to buy her love?

His chest tightened. No. He'd sacrifice a lot for Holly, but never that. He wouldn't cheapen or sully the memory of her any further. He'd cling onto the good times they'd had and pretend she'd been sincere in her affection toward him.

She sighed softly. "Please don't do this."

He pinched his lips together and clenched his jaw. And like a cornered, wild animal he growled, "I'm Sheikh of Imbranak. I do what I want when I want."

"Then I guess I was right the first time about you. Despite your powerful title you're weak and use alcohol to get you through life whenever things get tough."

Guilt surged, outstripping any pride he might have about anyone eavesdropping. Why should he care about what others thought when Holly sounded hurt and resigned to the fact she'd been right all along about him?

She sniffed inelegantly. "I'm only surprised you don't have some floozy hanging off you."

He downed a couple more drinks, then pointed to the shot glasses to let the bartender know to refill them all. Hamid threw back another three in quick succession. What did it matter now what Holly thought of him? She was leaving him anyway. And she wasn't shy in letting anyone know it.

It was his fault, really. He'd given her a month. He should have made it six. At least then he'd have had more time to make her see how good they were together.

She stared at the shot glasses, her face tight. "You don't have to do this."

"You're right. I don't *have* to do anything. Yet here I am."

He was being a dick, but her earlier rejection stung worse than a thousand bees. He was vulnerable and hurting, and he had no defense other than doing his best to drink himself into some kind of anaesthetized stupor.

"So what happens now?" she asked.

Though his soul threatened to shrivel and die, he kept his voice strong, neutral, when he announced, "Your month here is void. Feel free to collect your payment from tonight's proceeds in the morning before you leave." He lifted his glass. "You got your wish. You're now a free woman."

An animalistic sob threatened to tear up his too-thick throat. His hands clenched around yet another tiny shot glass. She didn't want him. She most certainly didn't deserve his affection. So what was with the tears filling her eyes?

He hardened his heart. He didn't need her damn sympathy! He raised his glass again. "Congrats, by the way. I hear you're a raging success."

She nodded, though her voice came out whisper-quiet. "You helped me get there a whole lot faster." She glanced around the room, her bottom lip quivering. "What a shame this is your way of celebrating."

His stomach hardened and fury pulsed. He was a sheikh, a man others respected and revered. And she was ashamed of him?

He grabbed the vodka bottle from out of the barman's hands. "Then allow me to remove myself from your celebrations. I need some fresh air, anyway."

Don't go. Fight for her!

He ignored that piece of him screaming not to give up. He'd already gone too far. He *was* a drunk. An irresponsible jerk. Holly deserved better.

He staggered through the crowd, his stomach churning at the many toxic perfumes and gaudy oversized jewelry. He'd been on too much of a high with Holly earlier to notice the very things he hated most, and now he was desperate to get out of the room before he suffocated or howled out his wrath.

Bad enough that every eye followed his departure. He managed to paste on a smile. His heart might be Holly's but it was the desert that called out his name, tugging at his soul like a benediction. A balm to his deep emotional wounds.

His smile hardened into self-loathing. He'd still give it all up to start again and be with Holly...his little flame.

His vision blurred, but he made out Dhamar as he stepped toward him. Hamid shook his head and Dhamar paused, then stepped back to give him the space needed. Hamid was only glad Jamal, Mahindar and

Fayez hadn't been able to clear their schedules at such short notice to attend Holly's exhibition.

He'd been such a fool to come up with the bet for all four of them to build a ballroom for the love of their lives—if it ever happened. Karma made sure it had happened soon after for him. That he'd failed to win Holly's heart had to be serendipity. Mahindar, the lucky bastard, had built the ballroom and gotten the woman of his dreams.

But though Mahindar and Hamid both worshipped the ground their women walked on, Mahindar didn't have Hamid's vices and abstained from drinking too much. He was the sensible, people's sheikh. Everyone loved him. Jamal and Fayez were also well-loved, while Hamid's people probably still despaired of him. This latest drinking binge would only prove them right.

He took a swig of the vodka, pushing past the crowd without acknowledging any of them. He didn't blame Holly for wanting to leave him, and though it hurt deeply he'd done the right thing in letting her go.

But he needed his space more than ever, someplace to drown his sorrows. He had a private courtyard, where he and any number of his harem had once had all the privacy they needed. Now he alone would enjoy its solitude and seclusion.

His stomach burned and everything around him dipped, then did a slow spin. *Damnation.* His recent dry spell meant he was no longer able to handle his alcohol. At this rate, what should have taken him a ten minute leisurely stroll to get to the courtyard would instead take twenty.

It was a relief to finally arrive. Stepping out onto the dark blue, mosaic-patterned tiles, luxurious cushioned love seats beckoned and water fountains tinkled, a soothing sound.

He hooked a foot onto the back of a hand carved, timber bench, and lifted the bottle to his lips with a heavy sigh. This place might calm his soul but his thoughts were still in turmoil.

"I knew you would come, Sheikh Hamid. I waited here for you."

Chapter Eighteen

Holly couldn't move. Her every muscle was locked into place while her stomach tumbled and turned. She'd trusted Hamid. She squeezed her eyes closed. Only now that she was free to leave did she mourn what she had with him.

They'd been happy! That he'd stopped drinking had restored her faith in men and humanity. But now...now she was empty inside. Could she trust a man who drank whenever the going got tough?

But then how betrayed must he have been when he'd overheard her rejecting him to one of his friends. She'd been talking shit, really, throwaway words that had been as much to convince herself as anyone else she wanted to leave.

She pressed a hand to her heavy, aching chest. *Holy crap.* She was falling for him. There was no more denying it. And she'd just blown it all to pieces by rejecting him.

Dhamar stalked toward her. "I just saw Hamid. He looked...devastated."

She nodded. "He thinks I don't love him."

"Except you do," Dhamar said with a shrewd look. "Guess you need to convince him of that now."

A man in a thobe approached them, dabbing at the sheen of sweat on his face with a handkerchief. "Holly, may I have a word?"

Holly frowned, recognizing the man—Salman—who'd been on the microphone explaining the origins of each photograph. He'd been witty and informative enough to hold the attention of the audience, and keeping the banter and information to no more than ten of the photographs at a time so as not to bore any potential buyers.

"Now isn't really a good time," she said.

"I'll be quick." Salman continued dabbing at his brow. "We've already sold twenty-three of your photographs, the offers coming through on each one have been far more generous than if we'd put price tags on them...so well done."

She managed a smile. That other people regarded her work as good enough to pay a high price tag was a compliment beyond compare. A pity the gloss had been dulled after what had transpired between her and Hamid. "Thank you. That is great news."

Salman nodded. "Yes, yes indeed. Now if you wouldn't mind making a little speech, thanking the guests, the buyers, and all those here supporting you—"

"Give me fifteen to twenty minutes and I'll be more than happy to do so."

Salman spluttered. "But—"

"You heard the lady," Dhamar interjected. "She has some personal matters to attend to first. Then she'll be back to do what needs to be done."

Salman bowed and retreated back to his microphone, and Holly sent Dhamar a shaky smile. She really was doing what needed to be done. Saving her relationship with Hamid. She wouldn't consider any other option now. She wanted Hamid. They were perfect for one another. She wouldn't jeopardize that ever again. Not even for her independence.

Her freedom meant nothing if she wasn't happy.

She needed to fix this.

But where had Hamid gone? She needed to find him and explain.

Aisha approached then, her expression darker than a thundercloud. That she still looked beautiful was a credit to her genetics. Clearly things hadn't gone too well with the tall, dark and handsome man she'd made a beeline for.

"Men!" Aisha griped with an eye roll.

Dhamar smiled. "We're not all bad."

She huffed out a breath. "If you say so." She glanced at Holly with an arched brow. "You don't look happy? I expected you to be glowing with triumph. You're the rising star! What is going on?"

"Other than your brother drowning his sorrows?" Dhamar asked.

"No. Way." Aisha's face paled, her eyes glinting with concern. "He was doing so well. What happened?

"He overheard me telling Dhamar I was leaving," Holly said softly.

Aisha sighed. "Women *never* say no to him. No one has ever wanted to leave him. It must come as quite a shock that the one woman he wants in his life isn't planning on staying."

"I'm not even sure about that anymore," Holly admitted. "I've become so focused on my career and freedom I've never entertained the idea of doing anything differently. My future was set in stone."

"And now?" Aisha asked.

"And now I can't imagine life without Hamid in it."

Aisha blinked at her. "You need to commit to him one hundred percent. This isn't just about him. It's about Imbranak, too."

Holly's stomach kicked at the thought. A whole country might soon be looking up to her. Could she handle such high expectations? She swallowed. Better that than to never see Hamid again.

She nodded. "I need to speak to him. Any idea where I might find him?"

Aisha stroked under her chin. "Actually, yes."

It didn't take Holly long to find the courtyard. It was ingenious the way it was tucked inside the U-shaped number of guest bedrooms, which were probably the old harem quarters. Little wonder he'd come here, and hopefully not for the memories. Plants and date palms in huge pots were strategically placed around loveseats and benches, giving it a private oasis feeling, mosaic tiles in intricate patterns of two-toned dark blue giving off a traditional Middle East vibe.

A smattering of solar lights lit up various features while leaving other parts of the courtyard in shadow. A fountain splashed and burbled in a relaxing melody. But any calming effects soon dissipated on hearing a feminine giggle.

What the fuck?

Holly rounded a huge mosaic urn to find one of the solar lights illuminating Hamid and another woman. He swayed a little as he looked blearily down at Ranna, the one and same beauty who'd been his favorite in his harem.

Holly froze, thankful the shadows concealed her while her stomach plummeted and her breath dried in her throat. Meanwhile Ranna swayed seductively as she slipped her arms behind Hamid's head, then stood on tiptoe to slant her mouth over his.

Holly's stomach pitched, and she pivoted to slip quietly away. She couldn't watch what was about to unfold. She could barely focus on putting one foot in front of the other. She'd told Salman she'd return within half-an-hour. But she couldn't face anyone right now.

She most certainly couldn't face Hamid knowing he was about to be intimate with another woman.

She pressed a splayed hand to her torso. There was nothing she could do about the burn that was spreading through her chest. She'd finally opened up to the possibility of love and it'd come back to bite her.

She stumbled down a corridor, already half-lost and confused. Though corridor lights illuminated the way her mind had gone numb, blank. She was a mindless body with a breath and heartbeat.

"Holly. Is everything okay?"

She looked up at Dhamar as he strode toward her and said, "You look like you've seen a ghost."

She shook her head. "No. Something much worse."

Dhamar slowed, then crossed his arms. "What?"

"Hamid and Ranna in the courtyard kissing. I-I left before I saw them go all the way."

Dhamar's breath hissed. "You're sure? Hamid is—"

"I'm positive." She blinked up at him, her mind working enough to form a plan. "You flew here by helicopter, yes?"

"I did."

"Then you wouldn't mind leaving now and taking me with you. I don't expect any special treatment. Just drop me off in your city and I'll continue on my way."

He rubbed his nape. "That's not a good idea. You and Hamid need to talk first and work things out, like you planned."

"Plans change. And Hamid said I was free to leave. There is nothing more we need to discuss." She held his dark-honey stare. "Please, Dhamar. I can't stay here a minute longer."

He sighed heavily and pushed a hand over his face. "What about your exhibition? You're meant to be making a pretty *thank you* speech to your guests."

"Would you mind filling in for me?" At his frown, she added, "Tell them all the proceeds raised tonight will be going to Hamid's wildlife charity." She managed a shaky smile. "I want to start afresh."

"Women," he grated, even as he nodded reluctant assent.

That his remark was a direct contrast to Aisha's "men" comment made Holly giggle, despite her despair. "You and Aisha would make quite the pair, both hating on the opposite sex."

Dhamar slipped his hands into his designer trouser pockets, his jaw tightening.

Holly's eyes widened. So Dhamar really did have a thing for Hamid's sister! Of course he did, Aisha was beautiful and daring. They'd certainly make a striking couple. Did Aisha have any idea?

Dhamar rocked back on his heels. "My helicopter is on the roof pad of the guest quarters. I'll give a quick speech in your place, then I'm leaving. It gives you about half-an-hour to pack. If you're not there I'm going without you, okay?"

Holly nodded. "Don't worry, I'll be there. And thank you."

Dhamar exhaled roughly. "I only hope I don't live to regret it."

Chapter Nineteen

Hamid jerked free from Ranna's grasp, his stomach churning. *Bloody hell.* Her kiss had had all the warmth of a Popsicle, her touch as cold and about as welcome as someone pouring a pitcher of iced cold water over his head. At least the shock value had sobered him up.

He didn't want anyone but Holly.

Ranna's dark eyes peered up at him. "What's wrong? Are you having second thoughts?"

He swiped his mouth. "I wasn't even having first thoughts. You're not my lover anymore, Ranna. I allowed you to stay here because you said one of my security men caught your eye. That is clearly not the case."

Her eyes flashed. "That was my excuse to stay here and get you to change your mind." Her voice pitched higher, a whiny note that did her no favors. "I don't want to leave you, Hamid. We had a good life together. You were a wonderful lover who gave me whatever I desired."

"I treat all my staff well," he refuted. "Which means you have more than enough funds to find someplace else to live and perhaps work."

"You're getting rid of me?" she gasped, her eyes narrowing into slits.

He hardened his heart. He'd had a lot of good times with Ranna—with all his harem—but those times were in the past now where he wanted them to stay. "I gave you a chance, Ranna. Now I'm giving you one more. I want you gone by tomorrow."

"It's because of that redheaded woman, isn't it?" she snarled. "What does she have that I don't?"

"She has my heart," he said simply.

Ranna's face paled. "It wasn't that long ago you still had a harem and all of us dreaming about you falling in love with one of us lucky women. We did everything possible to outdo one another and get your attention. In the end it was me you chose as favorite. It was also me the other women came to hate. Only now do I understand their animosity." She took a step back. "I just hope this woman is deserving of your love."

Hamid watched Ranna turn and leave the room before he stared into space for long minutes, using the quiet to untangle his thoughts. How many women had he disappointed and hurt in his short life? He'd always rebelled against those people who thought they were superior and above others, yet he'd readily used his sheikh status to enjoy a select harem of beautiful women.

It'd only been once he'd met Holly that he'd started taking notice how his actions affected others. Pretending he was a desert rat and seeing things from a different point of view had opened his eyes. He was no longer blinded by his own importance.

Nothing mattered in life without being able to share it with the one woman he loved.

Whop-whop-whop.

The noise of a guest's helicopter rotors startled him back to the present. He discarded his bottle and headed toward the doorway. He knew now what he had to do.

He'd track down Holly and apologize to her, then he'd tell her how much he loved her. Even if she rejected him, stomped on his heart and walked away, at least he wouldn't die wondering. Better to have faced his fear of rejection than to always wonder *what if?*

He stalked back inside the ballroom's exhibition, shocked to find the last of the crowd wandering out and Holly nowhere to be seen. He scanned the room. Even his friend's brother, Dhamar, was nowhere to be seen.

He found his sister at the bar drinking a cocktail alone. She scowled at him, though he figured she would have preferred to direct her anger at someone else. "I think you've had enough drinks tonight, don't you?"

"I'm not here for alcohol. I'm looking for Holly."

Aisha peered up at him through bleary, slightly distrustful eyes. "She went looking for you in the courtyard. Didn't she find you?"

His stomach did a slow rotation, this throat thick and dry. "I-I don't know. I didn't see her. I was too busy fending off Ranna."

Aisha's eyes widened. "Shit. You don't think—"

"I have no idea." He dragged a hand through his hair. "I've got to find her."

He ran to their master suite first, hoping against hope he'd find her. Although all the clothes he'd bought her were still neatly folded or hanging in their rightful place, the handbag and purse he'd had retrieved from the red sedan, and which he'd brought back here was nowhere to be found.

He sank onto the bed with his heart slowly withering inside him. She was gone.

Chapter Twenty

Holly ignored the tingling at the back of her neck and continued at a leisurely pace through the Baraz spice market. She'd already glanced back half-a-dozen times and had seen no one suspicious following her. She'd taken to wearing a plain gray hijab to conceal her hair and a modest abaya that covered her body.

She was just another woman browsing the Al Muwait markets early in the morning before the sun rose too high and made the experience too sweaty and unpleasant.

She drew in a steadying breath. *You're being paranoid. There is absolutely nothing to fear.* Too bad her deep inhalation took in the scents of saffron, cloves, turmeric, nutmeg, cumin, pepper and so much more. The heady combination all but overwhelmed her senses, her stomach twisting oddly. Nausea swelled and her face heated until everything did a slow spin around her.

She pressed one end of her hijab to her nose and breathed slowly in and out, doing her best to avoid the most pungent of the smells. *What the hell?* She'd woken up this morning feeling off and had clearly yet to recover.

With the dizziness and nausea subsiding, she lifted her camera and took a few shots of the array of spices in baskets or placed in little piles on mats. But her shaky hands had her giving up on the idea, and she instead began to hurry back toward her hotel room.

She'd obviously picked up some kind of bug or virus and needed some rest. Since leaving Hamid she hadn't stopped moving from one town and city to another, staying no more than a couple of days in any one place. That she'd been able to keep travelling and working was thanks to the demand for her photos that had flooded into her business email since the exhibition.

It tore her apart knowing the one man who'd broken her heart had also set her business soaring.

She stumbled on a backstreet's uneven cobblestones and she slowed a little, more conscious now of her surrounds. A rug seller called out his wares from a little alcove jammed with colorful mats and rolls of carpets, someone's washing flapping from a line in the desultory breeze above her head between ancient buildings.

A dingy little drugstore soon after caught her eye and she entered its cooler interior as thought compelled. A woman in a black hijab and white jacket approached and Holly rubbed her stomach and did her best to explain. "Do you have something to stop nausea? Ginger tea, perhaps?"

She really needed to learn Arabic.

The woman angled her head to the side, then smiled and nodded, speaking fluent Arabic as she spun around and headed toward one of the many shelves crammed with medicines, creams, potions, pills and more. She picked up a packet and nodded, handing it to Holly.

It took Holly a moment to realize it was a pregnancy test and she stared at it while coldness hit right at her core and a flush of adrenaline sent tingles through her body. Was it possible?

Hamid had always taken care of protection. But condoms weren't foolproof. And they'd had an amazing sex life. Even now her whole body ached for him as memories played out through her mind. He'd been insatiable and generous with his loving. She'd never been more pleasured or more responsive to another man.

She'd been with him for almost a month—four days in the desert and three weeks at the palace—and it'd been a little over three weeks since she'd left. It meant it had been nearly seven weeks since she'd first been intimate with him, and that it was all too possible she was experiencing morning sickness.

Holly swallowed hard, then nodded thanks at the woman and followed her to the counter to pay for the test along with some teas that she guessed helped soothe the upset tummies of pregnant women.

She smiled and shook her head as she left the drugstore with her purchases in a bag. She wasn't pregnant. She was being silly, even a little bit fanciful. Yes, her period was late. But she'd always been irregular.

Besides, the last thing she wanted was to be a mother to a sheikh's baby. If he found out he'd take the baby from her and she'd have no way of fighting him. Not in this country, not with his wealth and power. Women's rights might be growing, especially in places like Imbranak, but they still had a long way to go. Men wielded the majority of the power. And a sheikh was nothing short of a deity.

Her mouth dried, her thoughts whirling. If she did test positive she'd immediately return to Australia and use her savings to find a house, maybe even buy something affordable—it was possible now thanks to her photographs that were in such high demand. That she had thousands of photos stashed on both her cameras meant she had plenty of pictures to sell.

At least in her homeland she'd have rights. Of course Hamid would have the best legal team imaginable, but she'd have a fighting chance. And if by some stroke of luck he never found out about their child, she'd make sure her child would have a wonderful life.

There were beaches galore, rivers and parks and pools. Her child would go to a lovely school, perhaps one in the country or a small town. She'd make a great life there, settle down from her wanderings and perhaps find another income source with her photography.

She was deep in thought as she stepped out into the bright mid-morning sun and smacked straight into the unyielding wall of a man. *Oomph.* Her purchases fell to the ground and spilled out of their bag, and she jerked her head up from the stylish white thobe in front of her to stare in horror at the man she thought she'd never see again.

"Hamid," she croaked.

Chapter Twenty-One

Hamid drank in the vision of the woman who'd haunted his dreams these last three weeks. He'd been out of his head with fear and yearning, and a thousand other dark emotions. That she was now in front of him, her vanilla and honeysuckle scent enveloping him, her glorious red hair shielded by a dull hijab and her curves hidden beneath a plain abaya, only intensified all those feelings a hundred fold.

This wasn't the vibrant, flamboyant woman who'd fascinated and excited the hell out of him. He ground his teeth. *Wrong.* She was still there, hidden away, like the brightest jewel inside a metal safe. That she was clearly hiding her features, hiding from him, offended him all the more.

Her trembling set his jaw to stone. He'd shown her nothing but care and respect. But then perhaps she'd heard about his complete withdrawal from his duties while he focused on tracking her down? He'd been nothing short of obsessed, had never been so damn focused on a task in his life.

And here he was finally rewarded for his determination.

That his people seemed to rejoice in his love for this foreign woman was something he'd never have predicted. All they wanted from him, it seemed, was for him to fall in love and settle down. His duties would follow.

Yet now he'd found Holly in the flesh all his faculties seemed to have shut down. His mind too scrambled to string together even a handful of words while the pounding of his heart echoed in his ears.

He forced his stare away from her and bent to reach for her purchases. She crouched and reached for them simultaneously, their heads cracking together like castanets.

He smiled with grim satisfaction. Surely this was a sign, some kind of subliminal message? This wasn't their first time butting heads and probably wouldn't be their last.

She clutched at her forehead and he automatically reached for her before he as quickly withdrew. "Are you all right?" he asked gruffly.

She nodded, but when she lifted her head her eyes were distant and her voice hollow. "What are you doing here?"

His lips pinched together and his lungs constricted. He'd hoped she'd be a little happier to see him. "What do you think?"

Her face paled and she looked away to focus on her purchases. He followed her stare. When she went to grab the packet closest to him, his hand shot out to beat her to it. He picked it up, his stomach wrenching as he read the item. He looked at her while fury pulsed within him and he growled. "You're pregnant?"

She shook her head, but there was almost a resigned, fatalistic look to her as her bleak eyes held his. "I don't know. At least, not yet. Not until I take the test."

He'd been careful with protection, hadn't he? Heat flushed his body as his muscles quivered, his throat almost too thick to talk. She'd admitted to being a free spirit. How many men had she fallen into bed with since leaving him? Acid filled his stomach. "Who is the father?"

She jerked her head back with a pained gasp. "Who do you think?"

"I don't know what to think!"

She grabbed the boxes of tea and threw then back into the bag. "You're a good one to talk, aren't you?" she said bitterly.

His eyes narrowed. "I never cheated on you."

She pushed to her feet, her eyes blazing. "Liar!"

"You dare call me a liar in public?" he said quietly, though menace was surely pouring out of him. No woman or man had ever dared to say such a thing. And none would ever get away with it. But instead of looking fearful, a flush of anger stained her cheeks and her eyes glittered as she held her head high.

"You dare use your sheikh position to intimidate me?" she hissed. "I was your equal in the desert, as far as I'm concerned that hasn't changed. Not here. Not anywhere."

Damn it, but he admired her. Anyone else would be begging for mercy by now, all too aware of what he was capable of. But a bigger part of him was still raw and wounded, and betrayed by her infidelity. That she'd twisted her dishonor to make him look like the bad guy quickly diminished all admiration.

But no matter his opinion of her, she might be pregnant and therefore vulnerable to the heat and their confrontation. "Let's discuss this elsewhere."

"Elsewhere?" she repeated.

He nodded, then placed the pregnancy test into the bag with her digestive teas before he signaled for one of his discreet, security detail to bring the car. "Yes." He looked her over. Had she lost weight? "You really didn't think I'd just let you walk away again, did you?"

Chapter Twenty-Two

Holly didn't try to fight him. What was the point? She was weary to the bone, and, in that moment, sick of being sick almost as much as she was sick of pining for him. She'd missed him. And despite what he'd done she wanted nothing more than to be in his arms while the rest of the world fell clean away.

Her hands clenched around the handles of the bag as a big black sedan squeezed its way down the narrow, cobblestoned backstreet, everyone stepping respectfully out of its way. The driver climbed out and opened the back passenger door, and Hamid waited for her to climb inside its rich, leather interior before he slid in after her.

She clipped on her seatbelt and leaned against the headrest, a headache blooming into life behind her temple. "You said I was free to leave, remember?"

"I did." He exhaled heavily. "But not with so much left unsaid between us."

"If it helps...I've got nothing to say to you."

Tinted glass rolled up between the seats of them and the driver, and she had no doubt it was soundproof and bulletproof. She might have laughed hysterically if it wasn't so much effort. All the running and hiding, the anxiety while maintaining strict artistic work ethics had finally caught up on her. That she might be pregnant surely only added to her physical and emotional exhaustion.

"Look at me, Holly."

Why did it hurt so much to hear him say her name? Probably because she'd reveled in his endearment. *Little flame.* It seemed like a lifetime ago now. With a resentful sigh, she turned away from the tinted passenger window, where the ancient, crumbling buildings were already giving way to modern steel and glass structures.

She looked at his unyielding face. At his brilliant dark eyes and sun-kissed golden skin. At his smoothly shaven face—the same freshly groomed appearance he'd revealed for the first time at her exhibition—when she'd grown used to his whiskered good looks. Both suited him. He had sharp cut, aristocratic cheekbones, an aquiline nose and a strong chin.

Her eyes widened and a rush of denial swept through her. His plaits were gone; his raven hair trimmed to a far more respectable length. She'd been so distracted by trying not to allow him to see the pregnancy kit she'd barely held his gaze let alone noticed his transformation. "What's with the new hairstyle?"

That she'd once thought of him as a desert rat was so far and away from the man who looked back at her now it almost broke her heart all over again. She'd fallen in love with that man and her chest ached unbearably knowing he might be forever lost to her.

He arched a brow. "I'm not the same man you once knew." He touched his head. "I might still resist wearing the ghutra, but I've left behind many other traits, including alcohol." His dark eyes held hers. "I haven't touched a drink since the night you left me."

She crossed her arms, as though the hurt she kept trapped inside would stay there. "The same night you and Ranna had sex?" She hated how her voice wobbled. How Hamid's eyes narrowed and a muscle ticked into life on one side of his jaw as though he was the innocent one in all of this.

"You don't really believe that, do you?"

Her body tensed. "Yes, I do. I saw it with my own eyes."

His lips thinned. "Did you?"

It took everything she had not to look away. "I saw enough."

He sent her a bitter smile. "Then you don't know the full story. I had no idea Ranna was waiting for me in the courtyard. She kissed me while I was inebriated and caught off guard. But I pushed her away and we most certainly didn't have sex. I don't harbor any feelings for her. *None.* I made that very clear to her. There's only one woman I want. And that is you, Holly."

Relief threatened to swallow her whole and then leave her a blubbering, howling mess. She swallowed hard. "So you didn't kiss her back? You didn't have s-sex with her?"

"Do you really need to ask me that? I was determined to win you over and do the right thing by you. Yes, I stupidly succumbed to drink, but I didn't come anywhere near succumbing to sex. Ranna's kiss did nothing for me."

"Even you overheard me telling Dhamar I was leaving and you'd be a confirmed bachelor for a long time yet." The laugh that burst from her lips wasn't joyful, it was sad and rueful. "I don't know who I was trying to convince more—him or me," she admitted.

Hamid blinked his ridiculously long-lashed eyes. "So you *didn't* want to leave me?"

"What does it matter now? You believe I might be pregnant to some other man. Guess we both have trust issues. And without trust, we have nothing."

"It's not too late to fix this, Holly," he said quietly.

"Isn't it?"

He dragged a hand over his shell-shocked face and she twisted away from him, empty inside, as the car slowed and turned into a wide, sweeping driveway. Hamid might be a good man at his core but was that enough? Was any man—sheikh or otherwise—worth all this inner pain and doubt?

Despite her angst, her jaw dropped as she peered at the majestic hotel that came into view. The hotel was a steel and glass building in the shape of a sail spread out in the breeze. It gleamed under the sun, but she could only imagine it ablaze with lights. The car slowed to a stop and a doorman stepped forward and opened her door.

"Come," Hamid said to her, his voice clipped and no-nonsense. Like what they'd discussed had been nothing more important than the weather. If it wasn't for his set shoulders and jaw, she'd think she had imagined his shock.

She followed him into a huge reception area where a triple-domed roof and skylights highlighted the huge gold chandeliers beneath. A cream floor with diamond-shaped, gold-patterned mosaic tiles added to the class of the hotel. Next to a dark cherry, solid wood reception desk sat a bank of elevators, while further along a sweeping staircase beckoned.

She looked up at him. "This doesn't look like your style."

He frowned. "I don't always choose to stay in a tent in a desert when I go away."

He continued past the reception desk and she blinked up at him. "Surely even a sheikh needs to check-in."

He keyed in a code at the elevator and a green button lit up. He pressed it and the doors swept open. "Not when that same sheikh owns the building and keeps a personal penthouse suite available at all times."

"But of course," she muttered as she followed him inside the elevator and it whisked them quietly and efficiently to the top floor.

Inside the penthouse suite she couldn't help but gape. From the amazing floor-to-ceiling tinted glass with views that went on forever, to the luxurious white carpet underfoot and the huge balcony outside with its spa and outdoor seating.

She refused to look at the master bedroom, she wasn't that strong and invincible—she missed the physical and emotional intimacy she'd had with Hamid—and instead chose to sit on one of the red sofas that faced a gas fireplace and mirrored television that took up half the wall.

Hamid nodded at her bag. "I'd like you to do that test now...then we'll talk."

Chapter Twenty-Three

Holly sat on the toilet seat as she looked at the test, then looked again. One pink line. She sagged, but whether from relief or disappointment she wasn't quite sure.

Either way she couldn't sit in the bathroom forever, Hamid would be sweating bullets. It was time to put him out of his misery. She pushed to her feet and swung open the bathroom door, leaving behind the expanse of marble and white tiles to walk across ankle-deep carpet.

Hamid was pacing back and forth near the patio doors, his head rearing back the moment he sensed her approach. He crossed his arms, his eyes narrowing. "You have the results?"

She nodded, then held up the stick with its single pink line. "You can relax, Hamid. I'm not having a baby...with you or anyone else."

His hands clenched at his sides before he reached for the stick, then gazed at it with unblinking eyes. "I was beginning to second-guess myself about how careful I'd been using protection."

She sagged a little. So he no longer believe she'd been sleeping with other men since leaving him?

"Clearly you've been careful enough." She managed a shrug. "I probably caught a virus or bug. Or perhaps I should be more careful eating street food."

A knock sounded on the door and Hamid exhaled, then said, "The doctor is here. Good. He should know what ails you."

"What? I didn't ask for a doctor."

He strode to the door, then glancing back at her he said, "It's better to be safe than sorry. Besides, the sooner he checks you over the sooner we can have that talk."

The middle-aged doctor walked inside with his black medical bag, a white coat that concealed most of his suit, and a red and white checkered ghutrah that covered his head.

She sat stiffly on the couch while the doctor wrapped a cuff around her arm and checked her blood pressure. Did Hamid actually think she was looking forward to their coming confrontation? She'd rather walk across hot coals than be tempted to admit to him how she really felt.

"Your blood pressure is a little high, as is your temperature," the doctor confirmed a few minutes later. He checked her pulse next. "Have you been feeling stressed at all?"

She bit her bottom lip. "A little," she conceded. "I've been working hard—"

"She'll get plenty of rest and relaxation here at my penthouse suite," Hamid said smoothly. "I'll make sure of that."

The doctor nodded. "Good, good. I'd suggest a week of good nutrition, rest and relaxation." He looked pointedly at the pregnancy test stick in Hamid's hands. "Nothing too strenuous, though with lots of TLC I don't see any reason you can't be parents soon."

Holly spluttered, "We're not trying t-to be p-parents!"

The doctor nodded shrewdly. "Of course not." He bowed to Hamid, then absently patted at his red and white patterned ghutrah before he picked up his medical bag. "If there is nothing else?"

"No, that is all," Hamid confirmed.

The doctor had no sooner shut the door behind him when another knock sounded at the door. Hamid said, "Come in," and a chef in his whites pushed a trolley inside.

It was only once he'd set the table and discreetly disappeared out the door again that Hamid proffered her his hand and drew her up, then led her toward the table. "I hope you're hungry."

"You know me. I've always had a good appetite."

He nodded. "One that matches my own. I'm glad that hasn't changed."

He pulled out a seat for her and she sank into the chair, her stomach gurgling at the scents emanating from under the cloches. Perhaps her sickness had stemmed from not eating enough? She'd been on the move so much and been so preoccupied with taking photos that she'd not made the time to look after herself.

Hamid uncovered the first dish and she gasped. "Burgers!"

"Yes. I thought you might enjoy some food from your homeland."

He uncovered a large meat pie next with flaky pastry, then two pizzas and a creamy pasta dish. There were also a few Middle Eastern dishes. Fattoush, shish tawook and kofta.

"I'll have to make sure there are plenty of fruits, salads and vegetables for our next meal," he murmured, his eyes sweeping the apparently unhealthy food.

She teared up, oddly emotional. "Thank you."

"No need to thank me, Holly. Not after what I said."

She took a bite of the hamburger with its cheese and salad, sighing appreciation even as she cut off a wedge of meat pie, her hands a little shaky. "Is that your way of apologizing?"

He poured them each a juice from out of an icy-cold jug then sat down in a seat opposite her, his dark eyes glittering. "I never knew I even wanted to be a dad until your pregnancy kit stared me in the face. I'm only sorry I questioned your morals and soured yet another possible celebration."

Her heart did a nervous little flip. She cleared her throat. "I'm not pregnant, so it's a moot point."

He took a sip of his drink. "I disagree. I was being an insecure asshole and I should have known better." He leaned forward, one of his hands covering hers. "I've disappointed you. I won't let that happen again."

She believed him. He was sincere and unguarded, his heart on his sleeve.

He held her gaze. "Are you upset you're not pregnant?"

Her pulse quickened. "Upset? No. Of course not."

"Really?"

"I once considered having an operation so that I would never conceive and never have to worry that any baby of mine would go through what I did."

"That's...extreme," he said gently, his clasp tightening a little over hers.

"The doctors seemed to think so, too. They said I was too young to make such a radical decision and said I might reconsider having children in the future."

"Are you glad they talked you out of it?"

She bit into her pie. It was flavor sensation. Peppery, juicy beef wrapped in flaky, golden pastry. She closed her eyes, but she couldn't hide from his question. "Honestly...for the briefest moment this morning I imagined a life back home in Australia for myself and our child. A normal, carefree life with parks and beaches."

He visibly stiffened. "You planned a life without me in it."

"I also imagined you trying to take our baby away from me."

He shook his head. "Do you really think I'd do that to you, Holly? I'm not the bad guy here."

"And I am?"

"No, your dad is. He might be dead, but the memories of him are still fresh, and dictating your life—your future—even now." He leaned forward. "I'm not your dad, Holly. I'm nothing like him."

She nodded slowly, tension uncoiling inside her. "You're right. You protect those you care about, you don't hurt them."

He leaned back in his seat, his hand leaving hers. "I would never hurt you, not deliberately."

She missed his touch already, craved it. But it didn't mean she'd let him off the hook. "Not even when you were going to leave me behind in the desert?"

"I would never have left you behind, though admittedly I did enjoy teaching you a lesson. I simply took my men out of your earshot to speak to them." His smile was a little dry. "I didn't want them to tell you I was a sheikh. Right from the start I just wanted you to treat me like a normal man."

"I did and I do. You'll always be my desert rat."

His grin lit up his eyes. "Just how I like it."

"Then I guess I'll just have to remember not to call you a liar in public."

He nodded. "Better to keep such accusations behind closed doors. My people would want blood to hear such disrespect."

She exhaled slowly. "So you were worried about me, not your pride?"

"If something happened to you, little flame, it would destroy me."

"You mean that, don't you?"

"With every molecule I have."

She reached for a slice of pizza, her appetite increasing as all her fears and insecurities faded away. "I have much to learn about your people and their customs, your country—and you."

He blinked. "So you're willing to stay?"

Try keeping me away!

She cleared her throat. "Yes, as long as you are willing to tell me about your past, the good, the bad and the ugly."

He took another sip of his juice. He clearly wasn't hungry. "I never wanted to be Sheikh of Imbranak. But I realize now it's because I've never felt good enough for the role."

She frowned. "What makes you think that?" she asked, before she bit into the pepperoni pizza.

"Childbirth killed my mother. Instead of all of Imbranak celebrating the birth of a second son, there was mourning and deeply felt loss. She was loved by all. My father could barely look at me as I grew up and my older brother never forgave me for taking away our mother. He often reminded me I should never have been born."

"*What?*" She dropped the pizza back onto her plate. "Your mother's death was *not* your fault!" Her heart constricted. "Not even the best doctors in the world can always prevent someone from dying. Please tell me you don't believe your brother anymore?"

"Ardon is no longer around to make me feel guilty. He died in a helicopter accident, making me next in line as sheikh." His gaze dropped for a moment. "I'm coming to terms with my past now. Sobriety has forced me to face things head on."

"So you're really serious about staying sober now?"

He nodded. "I wanted to do it for you. But I soon realized I needed to do it for myself. I needed to slay my personal demons."

It was as if a heavy weight lifted from her shoulders, all her fears allayed. "You don't know how happy I am to hear that. You're a good man, Hamid Al Wahed."

"And you're a good woman, Holly Petersen."

She winked. "Just so you know, I knew you were never going to leave me behind in the desert, despite my initial fright. I'm a very good judge of character and knew you weren't a bad guy."

"Even though you thought I was a desert rat?"

"In all honestly, I enjoyed your anonymity as a desert rat." She sighed. "And I miss your plaits."

"Then I'll grow them back."

"You'd do that for me?" She pinched some crumbs off her pizza crust. "Careful, Hamid. You'll have me thinking you really do like me."

"I more than like you, little flame. I love you. I think I fell for you from the moment I spotted you in the desert with your red hair, flamboyant clothes and sassy attitude."

Warmth radiated through her, but she still couldn't help but remind him, "Even though you said your heart belongs to no one?"

"I was in denial. I'd never felt this way about anyone before. It scared me."

"And now?"

"Now I couldn't imagine life without you in it." He stood and walked around the table, then crouched beside her chair. Withdrawing a velvet box from out of his thobe's pocket, he opened the lid to reveal a stunning diamond ring inside.

Her breath caught. That it was a precious little star-shaped stone and wasn't something gaudy and over-the-top pretentious made it all the more perfect.

"Will you do the honor of marrying me, little flame?"

She pressed a shaky hand to her mouth, then threw herself at him until they were both on the floor laughing and holding one another.

"Yes!" she finally managed to answer, and though her hands were shaking he managed to push the ring onto her finger, then kiss her knuckles with more than enough tender possessiveness to warm her from the inside out.

How had it taken her so long to realize that being with Hamid was her true destiny?

"Nothing and nobody will ever come between us again. I love you," he said hoarsely.

Her vision blurring with happy tears, she whispered, "I love you, too."

Epilogue

Six weeks later...

Holly sighed luxuriously, closing her eyes as Hamid massaged bath gel into her shoulders and neck while she sat in the hip bath, bubbles softly popping all around her.

This is the life.

Hamid chuckled as he poured water from a jug over her neck and shoulders. "You're ridiculously easy to please."

She smiled. Her husband—she still pinched herself that she was wife to such a great, wonderful man and sheikh—had the best hands. "If you mean easy to please because I chose the desert as our honeymoon, then I guess you're right."

"So no billion dollar penthouse suite for my wife?"

"I wouldn't go that far," she countered with an arched brow. "Maybe we can do that on our next holiday." She pushed to her feet, bubbles sliding off her silken-smooth skin. She reached for him, bringing him close for a long, slow kiss. She pulled back to say huskily, "I believe it's your turn now for a bath."

"The bath can wait," he growled.

She stepped out of the tub with anticipation squeezing her belly as he undressed, his cock hard and pulsating. It wasn't until he ripped open a foil that she sucked in a shocked breath. "What are you doing?"

He rolled on the condom, then laid her on the sleeping mat and followed her down. "With the wedding and everything going on we haven't really had time to discuss when we'd like to start a family." His eyes were unblinking and serious. "And yes, I *do* want a big family one day," he admitted. "But right now I want a few years just to enjoy you all to myself."

Her chest warmed and the pressure inside her eased. She wanted children eventually too, and after so many years of imagining life without them in it, it'd be nice to have the time to emotionally readjust her mindset. "Have I told you lately how much I love you?"

He chuckled, "Not for at least five minutes." His hips thrust forward and he filled her completely. "I'll have to change that, little flame.

And he did.

Want more Desert Kings Alliance stories by Mel Teshco...
The Sheikh's Forbidden Wife
She chose to escape a future of tyranny. He has no choice but to take her as his wife.

Sheikha Yasmine Al-Fasih will do anything to escape her soon-to-be-arranged marriage to a vile man older than her father. If that means sleeping with esteemed guest—Sheikh Jamal Qadir—and forcing his hand in marriage, then so be it. Better to live with the mistrust of a fair man than to endure a life with a brutal despot.

Sheikh Jamal is grateful that his routine business trip to discuss trade with his neighboring country's leader, Sheikh Zameer, is almost over. A quick overnight stay and he'll be on his way. But on finding a blonde bombshell asleep in his bed all tiredness fades away. Zameer clearly knows Jamal's taste in women.

When it turns out Yasmine is Sheikh Zameer's virginal daughter—not one of his many harem women—Jamal is gutted. He's been setup! Yasmine is forbidden fruit and he took a bite.

There is only one way now to repair the damage. He has to marry the girl. But it doesn't mean he has to like her. A pity fate always finds a way to have the last laugh.

Chapter One of The Sheikh's Forbidden Wife

Yasmine Al-Fasih slipped like a wraith into the bedroom suite that had been prepared for her father's esteemed and honored guest, Sheikh Jamal Qadir.

Her eyes narrowed as she glanced around the suitably luxurious accommodation with its sitting room, sunken bedroom with huge circular bed, the adjoining theatre room and bathroom with plunge pool. The only thing missing was a kitchen, but no guest was expected to cook when there were Michelin five star chefs on hand to create the finest dining at any hour of the day or night.

That her father kept five overpaid chefs never ceased to amaze her. It was so unnecessary when their economy had taken a huge nosedive these last three years. Even parts of the palace were bordering on rack and ruin.

But despite the fact they were an oil-dry country, her father liked to pretend they were one of the wealthiest countries in the Middle East. A pity he'd relied on the now failing tourism for far too long. He hadn't diversified and she wondered if he'd left it too little too late, and that perhaps even negotiations with Sheikh Jamal wouldn't save them.

She paused at the top of the trio of steps that led to the huge bed and its occupant, whose potent rose petal fragrance filled her nostrils. Yasmine wasn't surprised to find her dad's favorite concubine, Shakira, lying in wait for their visitor. Nothing less than the best was expected for Jamal, Sheikh of Ishmat.

His pleasure and happiness was paramount.

127

Although many of the old-school sheikhs didn't allow the women
of their harem to be shared around, it was becoming quite the fashion
for the modern sheikhs of some countries to enjoy the status and
bragging rights that came with giving esteemed guests a favorite harem
woman for a night. Particularly if they wanted a favor in return like her
father did from Sheikh Jamal.

She swallowed hard as all her hard won confidence drained away.
How could she possibly measure up to someone of Shakira's seductive
looks and experience in the bedroom? Yasmine might be considered a
beauty and royalty to boot, but she was as shackled by tradition—it was
forbidden for a man to touch a sheikha—as surely as her father's harem
women were by their looks and their sexual duties.

Yasmine's dad, Sheikh Zameer Al-Fasih, went to great measures
for those men who were more powerful than him. That included the
beastly Sheikh Arif Hakim, whom her father had ordered Yasmine to
marry in a little over three weeks. That Sheikh Arif was older than her
father and twice as cruel left her insides weak and her throat raw.

She refused to marry him!

The thought propelled her forward once again. She took the trio
of steps, her nose wrinkling as she inhaled the overpowering rose petal
scent, hiding her distaste at seeing Shakira lying on the bed in a
seductive pose and a sultry smile, one that disappeared the moment she
saw Yasmine.

Shakira sat up, her dark eyes flashing and her full lips twisting into
a pout. "What are you doing here? I was expecting Sheikh Jamal."

"Sorry to disappoint you," Yasmine refuted coolly. "But your
services aren't required tonight. You may go."

Shakira's full breasts quivered through her gauzy top. "Says who?"

Says me.

"What does it matter?" Yasmine wasn't above using her superior
voice to get things done. The last thing she wanted was for Sheikh

Jamal to arrive before Shakira had obeyed her marching orders. "Your replacement has already been decided."

"Replacement?" Shakira threw her mass of dark hair over one shoulder, her eyes that were lined heavily with kohl blinking suspiciously. "I'm your father's favorite. He gives me to all his important friends."

Yasmine hid a grimace. It turned her stomach that these harem women wanted to service other men. That her dad regularly visited his harem while his wife, Valentina—Yasmine's English mother—was expected to stay faithful, was even worse. Her mother was miserable and it made Yasmine resent her dad's other lovers even more.

It was an effort just to stay civil. "Yet my dad keeps my mother all to himself. What does that tell you?"

Shakira's eyes flashed, her envy of Sheikha Valentina all too clear. "I'll be speaking to Sheikh Zameer about this!"

"Go ahead. Though you'll have to make your complaint in the morning." At Shakira's ugly frown, Yasmine added, "My dad is spending the night with my mother."

Liar. Her father rarely spent any night with her mother these days. But it wasn't like it never happened. The occasion was just becoming less and less frequent.

But hopefully Yasmine's bluff would work and give her all the time she needed to seduce Sheikh Jamal and force his hand in marriage. She couldn't suffer a miserable existence with the old goat, Arif. Being married to him would be even worse than what her mom endured with her dad.

Although chaining Sheikh Jamal to Yasmine for life would see him hate her, at least he wouldn't deliberately hurt her. She'd done her research. He wasn't cruel. He was known for his fairness. But he wasn't a pushover, either. He was merciless when needed. She sighed. She would just have to learn to live with his resentment and whatever justice he might mete out.

"Why are you here?" Shakira asked. "You're not the usual messenger girl."

Yasmine glowered. No other harem girl would question the daughter of their sheikh. Though Yasmine didn't class herself as a sheikha, the title belonged to her. It was past time she remembered it. "Go. Now. Or I'll be the one to speak to my father first thing in the morning."

"Fine," Shakira muttered. She climbed off the bed in a cloud of sickening floral perfume and billowy, ethereal fabric, then stalked up the steps and out of the bedroom suite, her bare feet making no sound.

Yasmine exhaled slowly as the door clicked shut, her stomach tightening with a fresh batch of terror that threatened to change her mind. No. It was now or never. If she left now and yielded to her dad's command to marry old Sheikh Arif she'd be subjected to a life of tyranny and cruelty. If she stayed and seduced the famed Sheikh Jamal, at least she wouldn't suffer a lifetime of abuse.

Would she?

No. She bit her bottom lip. Whatever punishment Sheikh Jamal devised it'd still be a thousand times better than living with an ancient despot. She'd throw herself at Jamal's mercy any day over being abused and mistreated by an old goat famous for his shameless depravity and ugliness inside and out.

She might never have met Jamal but she'd done enough research on him and uncovered many photos. He was stupidly handsome. Little wonder women fell at his feet. His half-brother, who lived in another palace, was gorgeous too. She was only surprised both of them weren't already married.

She took off her jeweled sandals. Though it'd be nice to find love, she could live without it. She didn't have a choice. She'd managed fine for twenty years in the lack of affection from men, what was another half-century or so?

Lifting her hands she pulled free her keffiyeh and shook out her blonde hair—a color inherited from her English mother—then slipped off her abaya to reveal her gauzy harem outfit beneath. It'd been easy enough to steal. The hard part would be losing her virginity to a stranger.

She sighed. She'd be twenty-one in a few months and she'd yet to know the touch of a lover. It left her a little queasy and lightheaded knowing it was her first time and she had no real idea what to expect, other than being aware it would hurt.

Don't even think about it. You're doing what needs to be done for a better future.

She lay on the bed and positioned herself in the same way Shakira had been. She grimaced. How the hell was this comfortable? She gave up and lay on her side. The moment Jamal arrived she'd move back into the same seductive pose Shakira had done so well.

Settling onto the bed, she lay quietly. The silence ticked by and she sighed luxuriously at the soft pillow and mattress. A cloud couldn't be more comfortable. She closed her eyes momentarily. Jamal might be hours yet.

She promptly fell asleep.

*

Sheikh Jamal Qadir followed the male servant who escorted him to his bedroom suite. Though the palace was pure luxury, he couldn't help but note how the expensive furnishings were fading and a little tattered in some rooms, the beautiful pieces dusty and unpolished.

It was clear that Sheikh Zameer's once impressive wealth was fading, too. But then tourism had been brought to a standstill for the whole world of late, not just for those countries in the Middle East. Little wonder the sheikh was so eager to begin trading with Jamal.

After a few right and then left turns along wide corridors, the servant swung open a door and stepped aside. Jamal nodded thanks and walked into the suite, the servant then shutting the door with a snick. Jamal ignored his surroundings and headed straight toward the bathroom.

Thank heavens this was a short stay, no more than an overnight visit. He was already over the scraping and bowing of Zameer's servants. He pulled off his robe as he glanced at the plunge pool. It looked inviting, but then so did the double-headed shower. At least his rooms were adequate, with little expense spared.

His host, Sheikh Zameer, clearly kept some suites up-to-date to impress his visitors.

Jamal stepped into the shower and lifted his face into the hot water. His advisors had already informed him that Zameer's finances had been stagnating for quite some time. Though Amack was still considered a wealthy nation thanks to its pristine mountain ranges surrounded by endless desert and sandy dunes, which made it the bucket list of many tourists, the travel industry was fading fast.

Tourism had all but shuddered to a stop. Add Sheikh Zameer's old fashioned ideals that hadn't progressed his country forward and its people would soon be in real financial trouble.

Jamal lathered his hair and skin, then rinsed off the suds before he turned off the water and stepped out to dry off. Although his own country produced good quality dates, buying a whole lot more from the date-laden Amack while helping to keep the country afloat until tourism resumed—and even beyond that—would not only keep their nations at peace, he'd be able to export date liquor all over the world thanks to his handful of distilleries.

In exchange he'd live with selling oil to his neighbor for a lower price. Jamal would still make a profit. It was a win-win. Not that he needed the boost to his own economy. He had his thumb in enough pies to continue flooding Ishmat with wealth. But only a fool would reject more influx of cash, and it wouldn't hurt to add to his already prolific portfolio.

At thirty-two years of age he was already one of the richest men on the planet, right along with his half-brother and closest friends. They really did all have the Midas touch.

The only trouble with wealth and power were those who coveted it from him. It was only lucky he had a powerful alliance with his friends and half-brother, which safeguarded one another and deterred potential conflict.

Placing the towel back onto its heated rack, he walked naked out of the bathroom. Tiredness was pulling at him every which way. It had been a long day. Sleep was in order.

He froze on the top step that led to the sunken bedroom and its inviting bed.

Weariness slipped off him as heat rushed through his blood and he stared at the blonde angel waiting for him. That she was sound asleep mattered little to him. It highlighted an innocent quality that shouldn't be apparent being that she must be one of Zameer's harem girls.

It was now patently clear Zameer wasn't totally old fashioned if he was willing to share one of his harem girls.

Jamal's dick jerked and thickened, and he swallowed past his suddenly dry throat. She was exquisite. The blonde bombshell must surely be Zameer's favorite lover.

He stalked down the steps, a growl forming in his throat. He didn't make a habit of mixing business with pleasure. But he wasn't a fool either, he'd had a productive day, and tonight he'd enjoy his reward.

For your exclusive FREE story: Her Dark Guardian, and where you can find out when my next book is available, as well as other news, cover reveals and more, sign up for my newsletter: https://madmimi.com/signups/121695/join

Check out my website – http://www.melteshco.com/

You can also friend me on Facebook at https://www.facebook.com/mel.teshco

Or my author Facebook page at https://www.facebook.com/MelTeshcoAuthor

And occasionally on Twitter at https://twitter.com/melteshco

Contact me: melteshco@yahoo.com.au

If you enjoy my books I'd be delighted if you would consider leaving a review. This will help other readers find my books ☺

About the Author

Mel Teshco loves to write scorching hot sci-fi and contemporary stories with an occasional paranormal thrown into the mix. Not easy with seven cats, two dogs and a fat black thoroughbred vying for attention, especially when Mel's also busily stuffing around on Facebook. With only one daughter now living at home to feed two minute noodles, she still shakes her head at how she managed to write with three daughters and three stepchildren living under the same roof. Not to mention Mr. Semi-Patient (the one and same husband hoping for early retirement...he's been waiting a few years now.) Clearly anything is possible, even in the real world.

Want more Mel Teshco books?

Contemporary:
Desert Kings Alliance: series order
The Sheikh's Runaway Bride (book 1)
The Sheikh's Captive Lover (book 2)
The Sheikh's Forbidden Wife (book 3)
The Sheikh's Secret Mistress (book 4)
The Sheikh's Defiant Princess (book 5)
The VIP Desire Agency: series order
Lady in Red (book 1)
High Class (book 2)
Exclusive (book 3)
Liberated (book 4)
Uninhibited (book 5)
The VIP Desire Agency Boxed Set (all 5 books in the series)
Box sets with authors Christina Phillips & Cathleen Ross
Sheikhs & Billionaires
Taken by the Sheikh
Taken by the Billionaire
Taken by the Desert Sheikh
Resisting the Firefighter
Standalone longer length titles: (50k-100k)
Highest Bid
As I Am
Standalone novellas and short stories: (15k-40K)
Stripped
Clarissa
Camilla
Selena's Bodyguard (also part of the Christmas Assortment Box)
Anthologies:
Down and Dusty: The Complete Collection
The Christmas Assortment Box

Secret Confessions: Sydney Housewives
Science Fiction:
The Virgin Hunt Games:
The Virgin Hunt Games volume 1
The Virgin Hunt Games volume 2
The Virgin Hunt Games volume 3
Coming soon
The Virgin Hunt Games volumes 4-6
Dragons of Riddich: series order:
Kadin (prequel - book 1)
Asher (book 2)
Baron (book 3)
Dahlia (book 4)
Wyatt (book 5)
Valor (book 6)
The Queen (book 7)
Alien Hunger: series order
Galactic Burn (book 1)
Galactic Inferno (book 2)
Galactic Flame (book 3)
Coming soon
Galactic Blaze (book 4)
Nightmix: series order:
Lusting the Enemy (book 1)
Abducting the Princess (book 2)
Seducing the Huntress (book 3)
Winged & Dangerous: series order
Stone Cold Lover (book 1)
Ice Cold Lover (book 2)
Red Hot Lover (book 3)
Winged & Dangerous Box Set (all 3 books in the series)

Dirty Sexy Space continuity with authors Shona Husk and Denise Rossetti:

Yours to Uncover (book 1)

Mine to Serve (book 6)

Ours to Share (book 8)

Awakenings series with Kylie Sheaffe

No Ordinary Gift (book 1)

Believe (book 2)

Homecoming (book 3)

Standalone longer length titles: (50k-100k)

Dimensional

Mutant Unveiled

Shadow Hunter

Existence

Standalone novellas and short stories: (15k-40K)

Identity Shift

Moon Thrall

Blood Chance

Carnal Moon

Lightning Source UK Ltd.
Milton Keynes UK
UKHW040221240223
417572UK00001B/105

9 798201 987046